GUSTAVE KAHN

THE MAD KING

TRANSLATED BY

COLIN AND SUE BOSWELL

AND WITH AN INTRODUCTION BY

COLIN BOSWELL

THIS IS A SNUGGLY BOOK

Translation Copyright © 2021
by Colin and Sue Boswell.
Introduction Copyright © 2021
by Colin Boswell.
All rights reserved.

ISBN: 978-1-64525-075-3

Acknowledgement: The translators would like to express their thanks to Brendan Connell for his help in editing the current volume.

GUSTAVE KAHN (1859-1936) founded the first wholly Symbolist periodical, *La Vogue,* in 1886. His pioneering collection of "vers libre"—a term he claimed to have invented—*Les Palais Nomades* (1887) also included prose "Interludes" and he became one of the most prolific writers of Symbolist prose, extending his work in that vein well into the twentieth century.

COLIN BOSWELL studied French Language and Literature at University College London. Whilst completing a PhD he began his career lecturing in French at Goldsmiths University of London and later at the University of Kent, where he was also Development Director. He then created and served as Executive Director of the first European office of the US-based Council for Advancement and Support of Education (CASE). He has published books and articles on the French language and on Émile Zola, and his translations include Petrus Borel's *The Treasure of the Arcueil Cavern* for Snuggly Books.

SUE BOSWELL also studied French at UCL and for a time taught French at Goldsmiths. She then moved into university administration, specialising in external relations and communications. Later she became a translator for the Wiener Holocaust Library, and translated Arnaud Rykner's novel *Le Wagon* as *The Last Train* (Snuggly Books 2020). Her other translations include Marcel Schwob's *The Assassins and Other Stories* and Ilarie Voronca's *The Confession of a False Soul* and *The Key to Reality*, also for Snuggly Books. Sue and Colin live in London and Ouveillan, a village near Narbonne in the Languedoc.

CONTENTS

Introduction / 7

To the reader / 19
Prologue: The End of a Theocracy / 23
Of Misunderstandings and Tittle-Tattle / 47
An Invigorating Long Journey / 97
Gevehrstadt / 135
Parades and Catastrophes / 159
Perpetual Erynnies / 195

INTRODUCTION

BY the early 1890s Gustave Kahn (1859-1936) had established a formidable reputation in France as a symbolist poet and as a public intellectual. His experimentation in verse form, breaking away from the classical alexandrine, led to his indulgence in "le vers libre" [free verse], a form which he falsely claimed to be the creator of, that honour going to Marie Krysinka, and this was seen for example in his collection of poems published in 1887 *Les Palais Nomades* [*The Wandering Palaces*] that did much to establish his reputation. And yet it was just at this moment that Kahn, for reasons that are not entirely clear, decided to turn his back on poetry and to devote himself henceforth largely to prose fiction. This led to *Le Roi Fou* [*The Mad King*], his first novel, published in serial form in *La Revue Blanche* in 1894 and then as a book in 1896.

As a teenager Kahn had devoured not only the poetry of Charles Baudelaire but also the novels of Émile Zola. Despite his adolescent admiration for Zola and the fact that they would collaborate from 1894 onwards on the side of Dreyfus in the Dreyfus Affair, in which a Jewish French army officer was incorrectly accused and found guilty of passing military secrets to the Germans, it is clear that Kahn decided to strike out in a different direction from the naturalistic path seen most clearly in Zola's *Rougon-Macquart*, a series of twenty novels exploring the natural and social history of a family under the Second Empire. In Zola's series the views of the third person omniscient narrator are rarely revealed. In *The Mad King* Kahn's narrator is foregrounded in the "Prologue": "For a clear understanding of the facts of which we are here the impartial narrator, some retrospective historical information is necessary." Therefore, we not only encounter the narrator, but we allow the author to use a rather clunky method to impart some important background social and historical material to us, the readers. As the novel progresses we feel that the narrator is being ironical when using the epithet "impartial". It is also interesting to note that in his introduction "To the reader" the narrator tells us that the author of this book could be "a bad prophet or a bad chronicler". The reader is not sure whether Kahn is suggesting that the author is the narrator, or whether they are separate entities. In his introduction "To the reader" Kahn begins the plot with a theatrical metaphor: "The curtain rises here on a romantic tragicomedy whose setting and background are social and contemporary."

As far as the plot of *The Mad King* is concerned, the novel could hardly be called a page-turner. The forward movement of the narrative is frequently arrested by long digressions that allow Kahn not only to explore his social themes, to which we will return later, but also to indulge in poetic descriptions of landscapes, and in his manifest knowledge of and love for fine art. One key element of the plot is the progressive madness of Christian, King of Hummertanz. This madness is primarily sparked by two dramatic events. The first is the murder of his son Prince Max-Eric in Part II, Chapter 5, an event at which he is a witness. The second is an unsuccessful assassination attempt on Christian's life in Part VI, Chapter 4, when a bomb blast kills several of his courtiers. But the narrator has implied on a few occasions that Christian's mind plays tricks on him by describing to us in detail his dreams and nightmares. The other strand to the plot is the relationship between the King and his faithful Palace Marshal, the Duke of Sparkling. The narrator hints at a complex relationship between the two men, with both probably sharing the favours of the actress Nelly Albestern, and at a possible secret relationship between Sparkling and the Queen, Christian's wife.

But the reader has a clear impression that the plot of the novel was not Kahn's primary concern. Some facts are puzzling. When Prince Max-Eric is murdered we are told that he is the second son of Christian. Later in the novel we are told that Prince Otto is the second son and that he will come to the throne on the death of King Christian. There is no mention of a first son, either dead or alive. Christian's sister, Margarete, is sometimes referred to as the Queen's sister-in-law, which she is, and sometimes as her sister, which she is not. The critic J.C. Ireson thinks that Kahn may have borrowed from Shakespeare's *Hamlet* and *King*

Lear for the dénouement of the novel. Ireson sees the final scene as a pastiche of the last scene in *Hamlet* with the arrival of Fortinbrass being transposed into that of Siegfried Gottlob. He also notes the similarity between Charlotte Brontë's *Jane Eyre* and the scene in *The Mad King* where Queen Margarete tries to burn down the Château de Thieve.[1]

Apart from the Duke of Sparkling, the characters are not very finely drawn and generally lack complexity. Sparkling is shown by the narrator to have a keen interest in the behaviour of others and is therefore more interesting to us the readers. A good example is the scene where the King, pretending to be Count Muller, is walking with Major von Langhirsch and the two men are airily discussing theoretical military tactics having earlier revealed their lack of interest in and knowledge of art, whilst the Duke, in the guise of Baron Schulze, is questioning Dr. Vana in detail about a number of matters, including socialism. Many historical people are referred to either by the narrator or by one of the characters, and on one occasion Kahn has opted to introduce a genuine historical character into the plot. This is where Dr. Vana recounts the visit that Napoleon III made to the museum in Pohlstock to see the relics of his uncle, Napoleon Bonaparte, stored there. It is interesting that Kahn's description of the Emperor is like the one to be found in Zola's *La Curée* [tr. as *The Quarry*] and his *La Débâcle* [tr. as *The Debacle*]. Zola detested the Second Empire and the

---

1 J.C. Ireson, *L'Œuvre Poétique de Gustave Kahn (1859-1936)*, Paris, Nizet, 1962, pp 354-355.

coup d'état that had brought Napoleon III to power, but he did not portray him as a powerful tyrant, and Kahn also makes him a rather pitiful figure with watery eyes and a shuffling gait.

The Mad King is set in a sort of Germanic Ruritania, the name often given to a fictional quaint minor European country. The place names (see the introduction "To the reader") are clearly Germanic. It should be pointed out that the Kahn family originally lived in Metz in Lorraine, which is where Gustave was born, and which is close to the frontier with Germany. They moved to Paris in 1870, shortly before Lorraine became part of Germany at the end of the Franco-Prussian War. But it is also possible that the setting of the novel is based partly on the time that Kahn and his wife spent in Belgium between February 1890 and the end of 1895, when they returned to Paris. One critic, Rachilde, cited by Ireson,[1] saw Hummertanz as like a morose Belgium described with the cruel irony of a traveller from afar. We should remember that Belgium, with its activities in the Congo, was a substantial colonial power and Kahn's criticism of colonialism is one of the major themes of *The Mad King*. But Kahn clearly had Germanic states in mind and there are a few words in the text that are better understood with a knowledge of German etymology.

Precisely when is the novel set? This is not entirely clear, but there are indications. There is frequent reference to railway journeys on express trains, there is elec-

---

1 Op.cit. p.354.

tric light, and the appearance of or reference to several characters gives us a hint. These include Napoleon III, who went into exile in England in 1871, William Gladstone, a late nineteenth-century English Prime Minister, and Sir Henry Morton Stanley, the explorer who lived from 1841 to 1904. It therefore seems to be true when the narrator tells us in the introduction "To the reader" that "the setting and background are social and contemporary".

One of the principal delights for the reader is the range of themes dealt with and the ironical tone in which they are treated. The theme of colonialism is savagely handled. Kahn himself had been conscripted in 1880 and had served in Tunisia. The novel is very much in the French anti-clerical tradition dating back to eighteenth-century writers such as Denis Diderot, the driving force behind the anti-clerical *Encyclopédie* and a writer that Kahn hero-worshipped. Kahn's treatment of the state church of Hummertanz does not pull its punches. There is one episode, both comic and touching, where a novice nun, suffering from a disease that makes her belly swell, is treated by the church as though she is pregnant and when no birth finally takes place after a full nine months, she is simply cast out of the convent. There are moments where anti-Semitism is referred to—we should remember that Kahn was a Jew—but it is only lightly touched on despite the fact that the writing and publication of the novel overlapped with the beginning of the Dreyfus Affair.

The primary theme of the novel is the decay of the European capitalist system and the monarchical regimes that support it. In Part VI, Chapter 3 the narrator tells us "The axiom was that those with possessions protect the State against those without possessions." Kahn was becoming more and more attracted to socialism and he uses conversations between Sparkling and Dr. Vana to explore this a little. The cataclysm at the end of the novel presages the downfall of monarchies in Europe. Kahn was also very distressed at how military power, including executions, was used to suppress insurrection, and this is handled in some detail towards the end of the novel. Although originally a poet, Kahn is far from practising art for art's sake. A series of essays in a book published in 2013 make a convincing case that he was a committed or an engaged writer.[1]

Kahn allows his narrator to tell some parts of the story with considerable humour and irony. There are some moments that are very reminiscent of episodes in novels by Flaubert, of whom, however, Kahn did not apparently have a high opinion. When King Christian and the Duke of Sparkling are visiting Dr. Vana's museum they are invited to put on protective slippers. It is only gradually that it is revealed to the reader that these slippers are made in the local prison where labour is naturally cheap. The scene where the King and the Duke meet in the street at night, the King having just visited his mistress, Nelly Albestern, is a comic masterpiece. Neither man is where he is supposed to be, and Kahn handles the embarrassed conversation between the two brilliantly.

---

1 Françoise Lucbert & Richard Shryock (eds), *Gustave Kahn : un écrivain engagé*, Rennes, Presses universitaires de Rennes, 2013.

Kahn was also a prominent art critic and he indulges himself to interrupt the flow of his narrative with frequent, long digressions. A good example is the visit to the museum in Pohlstock which reveals an encyclopaedic knowledge of fine art. This is another feature that he shares with his hero Diderot. But the detailed knowledge does not stop at art and architecture, we also have a detailed description of the military equipment in the museum. Another impressive feature of Kahn's intellect is his knowledge of Greek and Roman mythology.

Finally, although Kahn the poet had decided to turn his hand to prose fiction, the result is a very poetic prose fiction. We have descriptions of landscapes fleetingly glimpsed through the windows of express trains, landscapes seen in evening light, the docks on fire in Geldwachs. The syntax does not make for an easy read. The paragraphs are long, running over several pages, with sentences interrupted not by full stops but by semi-colons. There are frequent inversions of word order which mean that the reader sometimes struggles to identify where the main verb lies. When one allies to this the fact that Kahn uses an exceptionally rich vocabulary, including neologisms of his own invention, it is not surprising to see his style referred to by the critic Ireson as "refined and convoluted".[1]

One critic[2] sees *The Mad King* as a "rather eccentric novel" ["un roman quelque peu excentrique"]. She

---

1 Op.cit., p. 355 [Fr. "un style raffiné et alambiqué"].
2 Vérane Partensky, "Symbolisme et comique: les premiers contes de Gustave Kahn", in *Lucbert and Shryock*, Op. cit. p.87.

quotes Kahn as having written in 1897 "There will be books for the elite, if the mixture of the study of symbols, of myths, of legends, of sciences, of philosophies, is handled in proportion with the poetic elements and the elements of action that are indispensable for a novel".[1]

The reader is obliged to persevere, but the final reward is worth the effort.

—Colin Boswell

---

[1] "Il y aura là des livres pour l'élite, si le mélange de l'étude des symboles, des mythes, des légendes, des sciences, des philosophies, y est fait avec mesure, avec les éléments poétiques et les éléments d'action indispensables à un roman." Gustave Kahn in *La Nouvelle Revue*, March-April, 1897, p.586, quoted in V Partensky, Op. cit., p.87.

THE MAD KING

TO THE READER

*I*S this a political novel? No. A roman-à-clef? Not that either. *And yet it will seem to the reader that they have heard of these emperors, these kings and these ministers. So they're living people! Yes and no. They are to some extent, and especially if things speed up in the direction in which they seem to be going at the moment, they will be totally.*

A single path will have at least three or four possible bifurcations in the future. So the author of this book could be a bad prophet or a bad chronicler, but is it not sufficient that there should be a possibility of future truth to permit a hypothesis to be arrived at? And these almost unreal characters, where are they based? What is this Germanic Hummertanz (dance of the lobsters), Krebsbourg (the city of crayfish), Gevehrstadt¹ (shotgun city)? Is it in Germany, near Germany? No, and yet! It's in that tragi-comic country which begins in the Ardennes Forest, borders Thuringia, contains Elsinore and the Hanseatic towns teeming with ships with their rich cargoes.

Bohemia isn't Sicily's neighbour but its capital could be Wittenberg where Horace studied, or Vienna, where

---

1 Shown as "Gedehrstadt" in the text.

Escalus was a judge. It's the northern land in the geography of stories, poetry and opera; it's the land of legend, but which has resolutely entered along the path of modern progress with its complications and its consequences.

The curtain rises here on a romantic tragicomedy whose setting and background are social and contemporary.

PROLOGUE

THE END OF A THEOCRACY

I

FOR a clear understanding of the facts of which we are here the impartial narrator some retrospective historical information is necessary; without that the reader would not grasp at all the importance of incidents that happened in Hummertanz, trivial incidents no doubt and not of a kind to upset European equilibrium, but the moral importance of which is second to none. The events in Krebsbourg, the capital of Hummertanz, without ever enjoying the fame of a great catastrophe (great because the states where they took place were vast) have nonetheless given to the thinker's sharp ear the sensation of that almost imperceptible clicking sound which presages the premature demise of a beautiful piece of clockwork. The consequences of the drama for which Krebsbourg was the innocent experimental setting will be incalculable. Did not Michelet[1] spend his working life hypothesising the smallest causes of the greatest effects? The phenomena

---

1 Jules Michelet was a celebrated French historian whose magisterial *Histoire de France* was published in 1867.

we record and the repercussions of which are perhaps more imminent than the zealots of the established order think, in all countries and all regimes, are, amongst the series of prefaces preceding and giving rise to changes in the state of society, these phenomena are of a sort to be classed amongst the most fundamental.

Les us examine the topography of these places.

Hummerland, after a long and deplorable history the annals of which are filled with numerous painfully borne invasions, with territorial Atreîdes between hereditary families, with grasping share outs and with divine right, was at the end of Napoleon I's military and cartographic fantasies divided once again.

Hummerwald was given as a bonus to a neighbouring power which during these long struggles had modified the national symbols of its flag no fewer than nine times. This nation's army was famous for its enthusiasm for shooting with all its weapons at point blank range at combatants whose most faithful companion they had been the day before, in the midst of the most inescapable setbacks of defeat; consequently this nation had been endowed when peace came with a fertile and well-populated region and the government which took over had been recognised by Europe as having the right to levy upon it all the taxes it pleased.

The annexed people had on the whole accepted this state of affairs, thanks to an excellent idea of a minister of the annexing power. At each of these secessions during the times of the great wars whenever the sovereign detected amongst his faithful soldiers mutterings about military honour, he had cauterised the moral hurts of the anti-secessionists with the gift (at no cost) of medals issued from his chancellery. As with each secession an insignia was attached to the unchanging national flag with a different colour, in the same way the faithful subjects were rewarded with the gift of a ribbon of the same colour as this insignia, with a cross hanging from the ribbon. At the time of the annexation there was a census of the new subjects; a calculation was made amongst the ruling classes of those who because of their age would have been in the secession camp and they were generously decorated with this medal. Thus Hummerwald was kept happy and peaceful.

The rest of Hummerland (that is, Hummertanz and Hummerkopf) were reunited as a principality under the paternal protection of a prince of the house of Silberarmen, which had been removed from its ancestral lands, i.e. mediatised, through the conventions of a great power; to maintain the stability of the new state of affairs they counted on the fame which Frédéric Melchior de Silberarmen, lieutenant-colonel of all the great powers and holder of the Grand Cross of the Chequered Fleece, had acquired for heroically defending during a famous battle the wagons of tableware and the food supplies of Emperors and Kings against the forces of the Corsican Ogre. Nevertheless, differences in dialects, some divergence of interests, adverse superstitions, a long habit of hereditary sparring and vexations between some parishes at the frontiers of the two provinces gave rise to some raised eyebrows on the part of the politicians; and it was no secret that

Metternich had said at his club, to his close friends: "I fear some Kladerratatsch[1] in Hummerland."

He was right, the victor of Verona; the union did not last. The people in Hummerkopf were unbearable. Their banks, boastfully called State Banks, did all sorts of business with the Bank of England and the Stock Exchange, leaving not a nibble for the Hummertanz banks. Mme de Staël, invited to give a lecture in Hummerkopf, was surreptitiously inveigled into not spreading her beneficent words before the Hummertanz people. The King of Prussia had invited the world's greatest tacticians to take part in a parade at midday on 1st June 1827, in the Invalidenstrasse, a parade to be followed by lunch at the Zoological Gardens and by a presentation at the Opera, an exclusively military celebration (Spontini's *Fernand Cortez*, performed by a travelling troupe); only Hummerkopf people were invited. This, and other small slights, stoked the fires of revolution and the Silberarmen dynasty was quickly returned to Hummerkopf; Frédéric Melchior was seen galloping at speed along roads bordered with deep ditches towards his faithful territories in the same—(by an irony of fate)—wagons of tableware and food supplies which he had previously saved, and which the Emperors and Kings had presented to him as a souvenir of his heroic day.

They went to the small court at Weinstubb-Hohenglanz to seek the new sovereign; he appealed to the powers that be, for it was he who accepted the

---

[1] Possibly a misprint or variation in the original for Kladderadatsch—a mess.

lowest civil list; his requests and a few remonstrances from employers were influential; the delegates found him in a quiet alley of the grand ducal park, alone and pensive, holding a life of Henry IV; the most touching outbursts sealed his acceptance.

The beginnings of Hummertanz as an independent kingdom were unremarkable. They quickly set up an upper chamber, a lower chamber, modest suffrage and other political measures. The businesses of Paris and London competed as always to provide the State carriage and its accoutrements at the best price and as quickly as possible; they bought the carriage in England but most of the costumes for the essential cavalcade came from Paris. As for the brilliance of fine arts, so necessary for an emerging state, it came in one go, ready-made from Paris. It was beautiful and brilliant; unfortunately the innate sense of economy of the Hohenglanzers, passed to their new subjects, meant they left it to deteriorate, and no less than a Renaissance will be needed to bring to life again in this respect this country so favoured above others. They obtained a branch of Rothschild, paper money, a loan; they imitated some of the military disguises of the great powers, to provide a future for well-off young people with loud voices and gymnastic aptitudes; they paid a few soldiers, and everything began to work as in a properly governed country.

II

IT is forty years later; the new ideas have done their worst.

It was a troubled era; the country dwellers, stirred up by the priests, were on the face of things diametrically opposed in their desires and grievances to the townsfolk who were guided by doctors and lawyers. Only the venerated Worshipful Company of Stockbrokers, who shared the most diverse personal opinions whilst belonging corporately to the religion of the fait accompli, retained some solidity in the principality whilst carefully watching market fluctuations and making use of them. The Company floated happily through the never-ending applause and the constant threats, protected for the foreseeable future by the law which, ignoring its activities on account of immorality, allowed it to avoid the accusations (profit-making businesses having been fashioned deliberately by distinguished professors of robbery), and busied itself impartially with the ruin of all parties. The savings of the clergy and those of the liberal professions, brought together by the warm welcome of speculation, became no more than one whole in the happiest pockets of the happiest speculation in the happiest kingdom.

The company was not only solid and stable, it had been at one time innovatory. Far from being a link between the great money markets of Europe, as the great economist Pittersay[1] advised it to do, it had preferred to follow the advice which the same economist had given to capitals which were longer established and had a greater number of inhabitants. It had tried getting involved with Spanish railways, gold mining in Tuscany; it had been tempted by thermal springs in capitals. It had put lines of steam trams across Europe. One of its most delicate operations there had been to appoint to head these colonising companies a trusted director who as soon as the shares had been launched pretended *in anima vili* to disappear with the funds; they searched, they initiated proceedings; the shares, temporarily deprived of guarantees, having dropped to a rock bottom price, the fugitive director calmly left the house of the main injured party who had generously sheltered him and taken him under his wing? his honourability? against all the pursuers; the business was settled, the director filed his accounts, the share price rose again. This director, the victim of a moment's loss of direction, but above all reproach since he had provided accurate accounts, was re-employed under a pseudonym at the head of new ventures. The telegraph carried its fake news to the Krebsbourg stock

---

1 It is not entirely clear whether Kahn has invented this "great economist".

exchange, usury flourished and the financial backers of the regime acquired total freedom of action. The Company obtained from the government permission to sell the land in the colonies, companies of slave traders operated on its behalf, and monopolies were granted to it.

In vain had the lively and dynamic Krebsbourg agitator, the brilliant Papegay-Garten, friend of the Muses, several times called upon Krebsbourg from high up on his soap box, from benches on public thoroughfares with the debris of their stalls which had been ransacked by schoolchildren, to turn away from the permitted but harmful vanities of the financial world. He had tried in vain to drag his infatuated fellow citizens along the arid pathways of logic towards superior protocols and treaties of theosophical morality. As soon as he got up onto his soap box and started to speak he was surrounded by friendly keepers of the peace, whose duty and pleasure it was to direct him courteously towards a public prison whose brickwork overlooked the urban landscape from its dominant position. The men on duty who carried out this function, having instructions simply to lock him up, did not muzzle him, so that the speaker once he had been removed from his soap box could still shout "Long live the Republic" from the ground, from the running board of the vehicle that was taking him away, from the depths of the obligatory horse-drawn carriage, on getting down from the vehicle, on getting down from the running board, in front of the prison gate and once locked up, through the prison bars, without the shady despot Christian seeing anything untoward, since Republicans in the country were rare and carefully looked after by the foresighted police.

He was fairly soon released and fairly soon he got himself incarcerated again in the name of the indefeasible liberties about which he burbled unconvincingly. This innocuous agitation had allowed the Hummertanz nationals to harden their belief that all the iron ages, bronze ages etc. of the planet had found their absolute fulfilment in the age of capitalism; that the age of capitalism which had laid the most solid foundations of their institutions was the definitive age and that they were, under the most paternal guardianship, happy citizens beneath the wide skies. So they instituted an annual celebration of reciprocal congratulations of a mixed non-religious, religious, civic and above all dynastic nature.

III

IN short, all was going well in Hummertanz; sinecures adorned with the same appellations as in the rest of taxable and tax-paying Europe ensured calm relations between Hummertanz and these powers, along with its good internal administration. The real living organ of government was the stewardship of the civil list, whose very devoted head communicated with the stockbrokers to achieve greatest good for the sovereign. The latter did not hold back from interacting with his subjects, either by competing with them in the economic struggle in the field of market rises and falls, or contributing to the nominal increase in the wealth of the country by buying up as far as he could basic raw materials. That created a thousand more ties between the dynasty and the subjects. In Krebsbourg too, when they put out the flags for the sovereign and for independence, it was standard practice for the gathered financiers at their banquet to raise a glass to the health of their noble confrère.

The great hall of the Palace of Commerce, the former nave of a deconsecrated church, that day was set up for a celebration.

Every day created by Plutus[1] there was a hubbub, there were howls, a running around and heavy-handed joking; the putrid tentacles of business surged up with a great howling; financiers tiptoed across the great hall amicably arm in arm with the clients they were trying to seduce; you'd have thought they were tailors' dummies sliding along on rails, expressionless (so that no one would suspect what treasures of information they were slipping into the ears of the unfortunate listeners); around these powerful nabobs their secretaries frolicked, showing off their multi-tasking with a pencil placed coquettishly behind their ear, not with facts at their fingertips, but notebooks. Sometimes a telephone would ring and a stockbroker would rush to it, then return with an inflated look as if magnified with even more knowledge about the state of the market. The secret meetings remained diplomatic until closing time. Then the powerful ones would put on their overcoats and leave, amusing themselves with some play on words, yet remaining dignified, like no more than distinguished mortals but burdened with heavy responsibilities, essentially a part of the Ark of the Covenant; behind them through the portico came a breaking wave of the small fry, the facetious clerks, dancing, leaping, bantering, with hoots of laughter, silly jokes, pushing and shoving, suddenly calling out to each other and recreating the classic facetiousness of students who, a long time ago, would have taken their exams in Krebsbourg. The patients, the clients, the victims were leaving too, less gaily. That day, the

---

1 The Roman god of wealth.

day of the celebration, the banquet brought together the pillars of national prosperity; their behaviour was dictated by their dress; satisfaction from demolishing the victuals reduced the crafty expressions on their faces; bald heads alternated with carefully smoothed hairdos, parted along a middle line from forehead to nape of neck. The ministers occupied the place of honour; their fancy official costumes were even gaudier than the decorated hall, with multicoloured ribbons and precious metals; around them, in order of importance, the bank chiefs and the banks' young hopefuls, tender heirs apparent, were ranked in front of their plates.

IV

IT was a sumptuous meeting of international roguery. The Minister for the Civil List stood up. By a strange Rhineland quirk this distinguished civil servant was decked out in military costume. A handsome silver and gold helmet, similar to that of Pallas Athena, was at these festive evenings the headgear of this trusted potentate. Fancy epaulettes adorned his shoulders and below his medals there was even room for a sword. He spoke:

"Gentlemen, the lofty thinking which rules Hummertanz and circulates like sap around the robust branches of its sophisticated life wanted the earth of Hummertanz to be free earth; free not, and I know you will understand me and will also approve of me, you who are the reserves, you who are the treasury of the fatherland, who are its savings and its famous mother's milk (to quote the words of Sully who was great precisely because he was thrifty). And free not, you would not approve of me if I said anything different, and all my past as a loyal servant would rise up in protest, free not to encourage that licentiousness, resulting from passions and frequently the least admissible appetites which tarnish with their notorious crimes certain of our neighbouring countries; but free with that sacred liberty which permits self-enrichment under the cover, in the shade, I might say, of the aegis of the law.

"Your sovereign, gentlemen, has understood admirably how much the lofty carrying out of his duties could coincide with care for his reputation in the future, when he himself, delegating the details to your proud speaker this evening, wanted pretty much personally (for His Singular Enlightenment overshadows any initiatives by his minister) to take charge and preside over vast enterprises which have established through a number of universal trade exhibitions the glory of Hummertanz, the glory of Krebsbourg and his royal glory which reflects upon us all. And so he was able, as he stepped down into the industrial and commercial arena, at the heart of the miraculous harvests of gold, to be at one with you all. Our hard-working labour force, so used to privations, so ready to sacrifice themselves to the higher interests of public fortune, showed him more than it showed others the extent of their good citizenship and their sacrifice. You, gentlemen, through your special talents and your all-encompassing competence which make you the currency's thoughtful communicators, you have always put to the service of His Majesty your promptness, your speediness, the almost diplomatic information which makes your profession, already so fine, even more noble. And you have always communicated everything you knew about the progress of political developments which circulate in the stock markets and you have worked with us to discover the truth and the openings they provide. You will not be unaware that this willingness to help each other is what makes the solid and resonant glory of the State.

"It remains, gentlemen, for me to state precisely what this celebration is about.

"Alongside our parliaments, alongside our institutions, immediately below the royal power granted by God and the will of the people, you are a driving force. Thanks to you, to your ingenuity, the gold of our homeland accumulates, leaving behind the prodigal and the imprudent. You guard it jealously. By facilitating the circulation of our fortune, by managing in your principled and, I would say, safest hands, the most generous pensions and the most high-minded habits, you communicate both the movement and the unpredictability of our resources which, without you, would be threatened with stagnation. You excel at keeping your personal fortunes untainted by any losses so that they remain the country's unshakeable propriety by means of the accumulated figures which you represent. What do a few personal calamities matter against this fine spectacle and these well-ordered balance-sheets? It is through you that Hummertanz possesses what a beautiful country must possess, a selection of assets which I will call, with your permission, financial aristocracy, and aristocracy means virtue.

"Gentlemen, I give you our health, to our splendour, to us."

The Minister for Justice got up; he was rheumy, weasel-faced, unsteady, but highly decorated. His purple robe competed with the ermine of his attire. He had the wisest side whiskers of the region.

"I too will speak to you, eminent fellow citizens, about liberty. In earlier times your business dealings and exchanges were obstructed by a subtle interference on the part of the State, and by a rather oppressive surveillance by the powers I represent. A few excusable mistakes were followed by severe punishments which Themis,[1] a slave to the letter of the law, was obliged to inflict on the victims concerned, weeping whilst hiding behind her mournful scales of justice. It was through being moved by this sad state of affairs that our sovereign wanted your activities to be free and without other controls than your own discrimination and your honour; this was a noble response to the criticism of some of the press, to the ranting of frenzied speech-makers. Since then the fortunes of your Worshipful Company have largely developed, giving joy, strength and stability. What does it matter if there are a few small accidents which your wisdom cannot prevent? Justice and Fortune, finally reconciled, are walking hand in hand towards lofty targets. Your good health gentlemen, I raise my glass to the King and to prosperity."

A white-haired old man gave the response:

---

[1] In ancient Greek mythology, a titaness, the personification of divine order, fairness, law, natural law, and custom, whose symbols are the scales of justice.

"Thank you for the lofty and eminent words dispensed to us by you whose voices are sanctioned by your talent and the royal confidence invested in them. Once again and from the bottom of all our hearts, thank you. They speak the truth, those wise men who showed that the soundness of our portfolios underpins the greatness of our country.

"We have worked, it is true; but without the friendly co-operation of the kingdom's powerful men, without the generous legislation, without that charming welcome which attracted fortunes to us, fortunes which would have been quibbled over without much consideration in less fortunate countries, we would not have been able to obtain that calm approach necessary for big business. If the company has been useful to this country by reorganising the haphazard distribution of capital, the crown has earned the goodwill of the nation by protecting its most steadfast directors.

"Gentlemen, to the King, to fortune, to our illustrious and eminent ministers. Let the combination of our strengths and our interests remain unified; that is the great wish one can make for our homeland."

After these noble words, followed by ritual outpourings in many languages (for there were present exiled financiers from all other countries) there was nothing other than effusive exchanges of individual happiness. The banquet ended as a market, for time shouldn't be wasted and business is business; it was a question, after a little work had been done, of retreating to bars, like the Alcazar and the Scala, where young and old financiers did honourable business, the former however greatly helped by the positions they had acquired, and the latter by the information they were able to extract from the former. The result of these enquiries, called tips, contributed to enhancing their prestige; they were cheerful, very cheerful, and before saying goodbye they chatted between dealings about the rumours going around.

Some madmen complained about not finding work in Hummertanz! How crazy, these people who wanted everything! If they were listened to it would be the end of business and industry . . . listen to them? No, stop their mouths! . . . Besides, the armed forces are there and . . . these madmen are organising demonstrations and that evening they were marching round the city in groups, like troops, with banners and flags! There was nevertheless some reaction when they learned that some of them, a certain number of poor devils, had been standing in front of the Palace of Commerce and that during the time they had been enjoying the banquet the people's hot-headed speaker had again been honoured with martyrdom, that is, with incarceration. In fact, the crowd outside was dense. Since morning the workers' cooperatives had been criss-crossing the city, preceded by way of a symbol by their delivery carts. The men who were involved in these trades followed them, singing, shouting their support and approval for how well things were going, and with frequent stops not far from well-stocked popular brasseries.

On this day of celebration the crowd was very diverse. Behind the joyful union members, politicians rather than reformers who followed the sacred carts, symbol of the future financial feudal system which one day would strangle the other, there came silent columns of genuine starvelings, attracted here from little factory towns to protest about their poverty. The big day had started quite well in the morning; the leaders had given the poor devils a prominent place, they had duly exposed the only real human misery that they had. But towards this wine-fuelled evening, things became more confused. And added to this element of disorder was the fact that whole parishes, agricultural parishes satisfied with their social status (they needed so little to be satisfied), had wanted to benefit from the beauty of the day, from the splendour of the feast, to stroll around flag-bedecked Krebsbourg. The parishes were there in their entirety, male-voice choirs, brass bands, women, children, benefactors. It was an endless blow-out, a war of tankards, and the country people wended their way through the streets, all the women, children and benefactors dancing the farandole to the sound of the brass band.

They were hardly disturbed by the demonstrators; the peasants treated them as colleagues, perhaps a little less joyful (for in the town one has a good time every day), and the corteges going side by side sometimes blended into one without noticing that they were mixing not only processions but purposes.

At the very moment when happy and content, cheerful as good digestive tubes, the stockbrokers were joyously walking down the peristyle of their palace to head off to the Edens and the Alhambras, a large popular serpent hove into view. It was multiform because of all the disparate elements of which it was composed. So what happened? Was there an imprudent provocation, was the populace (the one that was demonstrating) shocked by the luxuriousness of the clothing of these fortunate people coming down towards them? The fact is that the cortege stopped on its route in order to receive them, but not in a nice way. An abundant rain of punches fell on the top hats, on the comfortable backs, on the well-garnished fobs. And the irony of this fact was that onlookers from the countryside, thinking they were present at the necessary corollary to the festivities, at the noisy end of such a beautiful day, joined in tormenting them when, had they been better informed, they would have made common cause with these heroes of thrift. The financiers retaliated with malevolent and hateful fists to the joyful and robust blows. To some, the demonstrators playfully inflicted that sorry joke of tossing a man in the air and catching him as he fell in a blanket in which a little copper, or iron, or other hard material had been negligently placed. Overcoats were stolen from their owners and they were only given back in tatters. The black outfits they had been obliged to wear for this gala marked them out unforgivably to their persecutors.

And when the firm politeness of the police had succeeded in rescuing them, bruised, in tatters, bleeding, they could no longer contemplate, given their ragged state, heading off to the Edens or the Alcazars.

It was a terrible day. The next day the liberal and reforming press congratulated itself on this incident. From the depths of his jail cell the hot-headed popular orator declaimed that the last theocracy had received a fatal blow. And the State could do nothing to avenge these loyal pillars since the armed forces, as far-seeing as always, had only managed to carry out arrests amongst the innocent country dwellers who had become mingled with this affair. The authorities and pillars of society had to endure in silence the insult that the popular parties are threatening to repeat on the same anniversary, pushing their cheek to congratulate themselves and to invite neighbouring countries, in their own way, to follow the example they have just given.

As Hamlet said, and the Minister for the Civil List of the country of which we have just written a page of its history: "Something is rotten in the state of Hummertanz."[1]

---

[1] It is not actually Hamlet himself but Marcellus, an officer of the palace guard, who speaks the line "Something is rotten in the state of Denmark."

OF MISUNDERSTANDINGS AND TITTLE-TATTLE

I

THE KING rose in a foul, icy mood.
Heavy-winged dreams had glided over the palace that night. Frescoes of flames and looting had laid waste to the royal sleep. The roads of Hummertanz had suddenly been illuminated by reddish, ghost-like, infernal fires. And descending sharp slopes there wended countless peasants' carts laden with furniture, bristling with shivering old women. Cavalry regiments on the rampage were levying taxes on all the towns that could not provide a sufficient quantity of Japanese masks. As far as the Hummertanz infantry was concerned, these fine regiments of volunteers bought out of rural poverty, they were fraternising with the enemy in farms to sing tunes from operettas. There had been no doubt: the plans for mobilisation and defence of fortresses had been undermined by these conservatory musicians, who were so servile and arrogant, and who had tried in vain to exploit the Queen's liking for music, to damage the majesty of the Civil Lists, to dissipate and melt down the metal coinage portraits of the sovereign not even into smoke, but into no more than musical chords. It was these same men with their

lobster claws who had just played, in front of the palace walls, an ironic dawn serenade making use of the historic brasses of the royal kitchen, brasses which for the most part had come from Jerusalem at the time of the great crusades. And what damage to the funds of the State! The whole market was in tears.

Once he was awake the King reassured himself that he still existed physically. A few psychological investigations confirmed that his moral being was still in place. But what a drag, these dreams! And whose fault? This blasted Palace Marshal, the Duke of Sparkling, always keen to offer the King, with full orchestration of honeyed phrases and insidious proposals of amusing excursions, the first fruits of all the feudal vines, or of those of upstarts, even of vines growing wild. It was thanks to him that King Christian had allowed himself to be enrolled in the Thousand and One Nights Club, a club specially reserved for reigning monarchs and other members proposed by monarchs. The club had premises in all capital cities, with cordial and devoted tour guides from around the world with the most up-to-date local knowledge. The club was a centre of amusing but expensive entertainment.

The King thinks sadly about the phrases that had taken him in. What a mistake to believe that Haroun-al-Raschid strolled around in the streets of Baghdad and Basra to dispense justice and listen to tales! What a mistake to believe that when Peter the Great was working wood he was thinking only of the navy and the reconstruction of the Eastern Empire! And in the case of Joseph II, do you think that Casanova could have recounted to him his interesting anecdotes, if Joseph himself, in the company of this amoral escapee, had not visited a few shady dives of his capitals and cheered up his august brow in not particularly decent society? And who was Shakespeare thinking of in *Measure for Measure* which has just been performed for us? Of no one in particular, may one say? But finally, although poets, in truth, recollect more than they invent, and hasten most often to reedit the sayings, the moral features and adventures of the eminent people that they were allowed to meet one evening, should one not see in this a prophetic insight, a valid reason produced for public consumption to justify the absences of princes, beyond the confines of their domain? This idea of justice had always been excellent and normal from the most bygone times, this opinion had been left to him unintentionally by someone whose rank one could not know precisely but was definitely highly placed "perhaps not far from the steps of the throne but definitely not Hamlet, this poor Hamlet, a schemer, a sentimental man, a myth." And smiling at his own jokes the Duke, having jovially falsified a few historical facts, had boosted in the eyes of the sovereign the reputation of this brilliant Henry IV, still adored by the republicans of France, this valiant king, this playboy. "As far as Henry IV was concerned how was it that he left this brilliant trail, this glorious reputation, stained perhaps only a little by a few anecdotes which might allow one to give him the familiar appellation of a party animal? It was because he had an excellent Minister for the Civil List, his famous Sully." King Christian had a

Sully. Hummertanz was awash with capable Sullys; the King quickly learned to control them and knew how to inspire them with a few words. Moreover, without wishing to elevate himself by any comparison to the level of any of the companions of Henry IV, the Duke of Sparkling felt that his noble role in life would be to be the zealous acolyte of the King in that luxurious part of his fine existence which he allowed himself to reveal to the King. It would be he who took care that the memory of his sovereign should be surrounded by charm in the eyes of the descendants of his actual subjects and thus saw himself contributing for the most part to the good of the dynasty, its soundness and its wellbeing.

The King had believed his faithful servant. A few festivities in neighbouring capitals involved him in the majority of innocent games. Sparkling was really funny in the unexpected rude sketches played in the funfairs, the carnival imbroglios and the whole repertoire of farces with which one may victimise the venerable and clumsy intellectuals.

But it was expensive and tiring, intoxicating and heavy; after the feast came the bad dream. The Sully of Hummertanz, understandably uneasy about Sparkling's influence (in a few minutes and having been drinking, one could have signed treaties with foreign powers, commercial agreements and even stock exchange orders), had fought back heroically and without hesitation; he was not asking for asceticism, but care with expenditure, not pure wisdom but a delicate choice of pleasures. Tender so as to be persuasive, he had soberly indicated that simple promises coming from on high could advantageously replace the too gross freedoms demanded of the distinguished members, masked in shade and anonymity, of the Thousand and One Nights Club. This argument had struck the eyes of the sovereign with the serene certainty of an axiom. Christian had seen again the gardens of paradise. And thus the Minister for the Civil List became almost certain of the imminent disgrace of his rival. Henceforth, without abusing his privileges, he had discredited again and again and placed under the eyes of his sovereign a hand-written letter he had acquired at auction in a lot of personal revelations. It went: "A thousand thanks, my dear Duke, but I found my bag as I got out of my coach yesterday evening."[1] The King had recognised the handwriting and the style, the name on the envelope and the signature, but without fully understanding the meaning. It was no doubt mysterious, allusive, perhaps not clear but, in any case, it could not mean anything good was coming. Building insinuation upon insinuation the Great Economist had allowed the man he wished to be prosperous and respected among all others to glimpse that the noble and profound mark of respect addressed to the Duchess of Sparkling, spiced up if necessary with a few revelations about the rather eclectic, too facile and duplicitous character that was the Duke, could constitute where the good of the State and its Living

---

[1] There are two grammatical errors in this sentence in the original text, which no doubt helped the King to identify the writer.

Representative were concerned, a necessary, skilful and advantageous manoeuvre. At this point it was not possible to be certain that the first approaches were completely unsuccessful. King Christian regained a little gaiety and was only a little sarcastic[1] in the depths of this soul at the time when, fully awake and dressed in his little uniform, he carried out each morning his inspection of the palace. This palace was comfortable but plain, similar as far as had been possible externally to the Banque de France and internally to the apartments of a good, thrifty millionaire living in some distant province. The purpose of this regular ambulation: to assure himself that from dawn onwards everything had been rubbed, dusted, polished, that the decorative pots, the leather book covers had not been displaced; to assure himself also that no one had walked on the carpets woven by the ladies of the towns, industrious and loyal versions of Arachne.[2] Fearing damage and dust, he was the only person who could see clearly in the furnishing and administrative darkness and so he wished to cast his masterly eye everywhere. The Palace Marshal was coming, it was time to cut him down to size.

---

1 The verb used by Kahn in the text "sarcasticiser" is a neologism not found in the *Trésor de la Langue Française*.
2 In his *Metamorphoses* Ovid recounts how the talented mortal Arachne challenges the goddess Minerva to a weaving contest. Arachne won the competition but later hanged herself out of shame and was turned into a spider.

II

THE express train was carrying away an ill-tempered and rather surprised Sparkling. Why this haste to send him off, a special courier (when so many couriers were available), the bearer of special sealed letters to this small sister state, with which epistolary relations could be adequate on a daily basis. What private affair could the King have which had to remain so secret, or what political business on this trouble-free horizon? Was he the noble instrument of some intrigue ending in conspiracies with some other great and terrifying power of whom his hosts of tomorrow were taking pride in being the harmless allies? Or was he simply going to bring back yet another decoration? What would be the point of that! Were they preparing to play some coarse trick on him as they did at the club? But no! The King was too good and, anyway, on his own, could he have invented some coarse trick without the help of his faithful Sparkling. Unlikely—really unlikely! Had everything not seemed so normal when he left? The Duchess had that air of resigned victim that she had whenever her husband left. He had briefly bumped into his colleague for the civil list and the latter had on his face that inimical and roguish expression that he had at the sight of his dear Marshal. No, it was not exile and certainly not a bad joke and so the business could not be urgent. A whim of the King; is he going to rule on his own over anything other than his personal interests? Absurd! Absurd! The Duke undid some papers.

The express was passing through fertile plains criss-crossed by waterways; landscapes were passing by looking like small varnished pictures. Sometimes nature made doubtless mad errors of perspective. Sparkling, who travelled rarely by day, was interested when the train cut through a village, strident, whistling, making a din[1] only a metre away from the doors of inns where suddenly surprised faces gazed wide-eyed. A village, a town hall, a factory then a puddle and a pasture. One could hear the laughter of the travelling women and girls when the sight of dainty objects got smaller, sheep in the distance, hens pecking, the pastorals that were the embankments of the small stations. The empty but terrified eyes of the peasants sitting on their baskets admired the speed of this expensive train. In iron and glass stations, vibrating with the noise, the screaming express desperately jolted its ironwork, like an important person tinkling their trinkets, and shrill carillons of bells continued. In sidings impressive trains of

---

1 The word "brouant" in Kahn's original text is not in the *Trésor de la Langue Française*.

workmen's convoys disgorged a jostling, hairy crowd of men with square jaws,[1] heavy feet, with a gait that was more swinging than that of townspeople. A few memories of a different life came back to him when his escapades were more youthful and his pleasures more naïve. Hummertanz ceased to exist. At ease thanks to his diplomatic immunity, the Duke saw people being harassed by the customs officers of the neighbouring country; a different dialect could be heard; the different uniforms of the policemen showed that one was no longer in the sweet home country. And amongst the crowd milling around on the platform, tired of the spies and the questions, only the railway employees, busy, hurrying about, running hither and thither to no purpose, seemed perfectly at ease, ordinary migrants who had nothing to do with the customs officers. Sparkling noted how much this practice of not searching the luggage of the railway employees offered a large scope for contraband. And because as habitual travellers they raised no suspicions, did it not necessarily follow that these employees should increase their salary through a few thefts, a few minor infringements of customs duties? It was an idea, and what would the Minister for Railways think when, one day, during a council meeting, Sparkling would set out this simple point of view, this not very important, but ingenious, Christopher Columbus' egg[2] with a tiny America, a

---

1 This is an approximate translation as two words are totally unreadable in the printed facsimile French text.
2 The reference to "l'oeuf de Colomb" is the origin of an expression meaning "a simple but obvious solution". The story is that

tiny galleon.

This Minister was so open to be the butt of jokes and this was a good one. This ascetic engineer! His involuntary funny behaviour amused the Duke. Did he not stop all trains running on Sunday, this pious fellow, doubtless so that his civil servants could freely go to the inn and prepare the derailments for Monday? Had he not had the brilliant idea to forbid his wagons and lorries to transport anything he judged to be immoral, and just how many things may appear immoral to the man who walks with his gaze lowered and his hands in his sleeves like a prude. And just the sight of Sparkling's gaiety was enough to mutate the waxy yellow tones of his face into a light blush. And the joy for Sparkling at those moments was to be entrepreneurial, risqué, daring, enticing, dancing about whilst letting slip references to a number of unserious newspapers, not transportable according to the railway man, vital to be transported according to the Palace Marshal. One thing will kill the other: the railway minister, this fierce adversary of jollity, must be decked out in brocade and Sparkling had a fleeting sense of jollity.

Nevertheless the countryside he was travelling through became pale and sad. The sand formed reddish dunes; too compact artificial-looking pine-groves spoiled the horizon. From the approach of twilight a watery sadness spreads and comes to the level of the misty soil, thin cattle are returning home, small

---

Columbus challenged his crew to balance a hard-boiled egg. They failed. But Columbus smashed one end of his egg and the egg remained upright.

hares are fleeing round the bends in paths. The small towns reveal from a distance a little of their slate bell towers, well away from their railway station, that sign of anti-civilisation. And from this sky becoming more misty and grey as the distant features become swollen with blackish rainy steam, increased melancholy invades this train that trots along now as a slumping little old lady, noiselessly, like a little old bag-carrying woman, running along in this poor country as though in the embrace of poverty. Ah! What boredom! What boredom! To sleep a deep sleep, read either the English or French novel bought in the station. Read! He, Sparkling, this joyful companion, read anything other than what was vital or the world's newspapers. Ah, no. Never.

And the purpose of his mission returned to torture his mind again. "A political or a personal affair, that cannot be so urgent, we will stop at the next big city and set out again tomorrow morning."

III

AH! What bad luck! The town of Lachenfels is but sadness and gloom. The faithful Wilhelm, that excellent friend who it would have been such a pleasure to see, has left that very morning, taking to another residence the sickly Princess to whom he is both mentor and keeper. "All her caprices, not a single one of her wishes," this was the task imposed on faithful Wilhelm by the Prince who entrusted him with the task of keeping from his old and drily polite but not surly wife harmful and foreign literary influences, whilst keeping him (one wonders why?) at immeasurable distances. "I am going to see my wife, let her know and prepare for her that chestnut Mont-Blanc she likes so much and get her ice-cream makers ready," the illustrious Prince had said one evening, the most famous of his evenings of jollity, and it was possibly his only funny phrase, even though its paternity has been disputed behind many discreet smiles. Recently there were vestiges of a perfume of Persian lilac in the private staircase of the princely dwelling, on the Prince's side—a side that was totally separated from that of the Princess by a large courtyard that was enlivened by the presence of a sentry and of a melancholic drum sitting in front of the guard house. A word, a perfume, they had got tongues wagging, all the more so as the following day Pastor Manlius Tocker, summoned to the palace, spent two whole hours in the Prince's office, known as the Steel Office, famous for its ornaments, its arrays of precious old sabres and masses of arms decorating the whole wall. It was the rhythm of a few old days of youth that had returned just once after so many years. A perfume, a joke and the following day the pastor, it was the ordinary pace of yesteryear. Moreover, this time, two days later, there was a major military review and presentation of a quarter-master-major general.

As for the sickly Princess, for many years her sole pleasure had been to invite the oldest titled ladies in Europe to come and see her; sipping teas served in special Sèvres porcelain cups, aged ladies, landslides of grey and accumulated centuries spoke of the beauty of death, and the edifying disappearance of their ancestors; these were the happy evenings, the tea parties imbued with a calm charm; on the other hand, when the final descendant of a noble family, and not even a related one, had faltered, it was a sad tea party, full of lamentations and a foretaste of grief for a few days. And even if sometimes the descendant of some lofty race had to be placed under power of attorney, the court went into mourning for one evening. The Princess was entirely given over to serious, pious memories, and she had a maternal affection for the whole nobility of Europe, except for her august husband whom she had never in any respect been able to stomach. And so faithful Wilhelm vegetated in this solemn setting; but sometimes, too rarely but as frequently as possible, what fine outings to see dear old Sparkling, and to wage war with him on some fine bottles of French wine.

No tea, no tea, my dear friend, do you not understand there will be no tea this evening! Wilhelm radiated like an apotheosis; then he set off for Lachenfels which the Princess had chosen amongst other palaces since the Prince never came there. In the end, if Wilhelm is not there, the general who commands the town is his friend; Sparkling knows him and an hour of military jollity (maybe not as good as civilian jollity) could still be an amusement! But no, the general is not there either; at the express orders of his bellicose sovereign he has been sent as the bearer of a bombastic toast that he has to repeat word for word in the officers' mess of a neighbouring town; but, so said the duty officer, the general will be back tomorrow for he is so fond of Lachenfels; one could send him a telegram; it would be just the excuse he needed to leave the town where he was holding forth, for he does not like to hang about at these meetings of subordinates. He knows only too well that he is stopping them continuing their daily games. He would not admit so much, but he would be delighted to be recalled. Sparkling hesitates, thinks up reasons, refuses; he knows that, on these occasions, the general, aggrandised by the royal speech he has just pronounced, would be too magnificently serious.

Nothing, no distractions; in the theatre that blasted Viennese operetta. Downcast he sets off on his own.

Waltzes drift languorously from windows bedecked with flowers, pairs of officers make their sabres ring against the paving stones of the street, the waltzes stop. From the flower-covered windows young faces speak a few words to them, then there is laughter; the sabres trail along and the waltz fades away. The closed public houses seem philosophical. He is watched from the doors of small food shops; the slow walking pace of an important foreigner excites curiosity and soon urchins approach him timidly. Would Sir like a guide to visit the castle, to see the promenade alongside the river? The Duke pushes them gently aside to begin with, then with some irritation, he loses his temper and escapes from these empty districts that contain no doubt the most populous streets of Lachenfels. He walks quickly and is soon, feverishly and alone, striding through anonymous streets, past small white houses with yellow wooden verandas, with flower-covered windows from which waltzes are pouring, from which lieder are floating, and everything is closed, and everything is instinct, and everything is forget-me-not, apart from Sparkling who is furious. A solitary dinner, a melancholic dinner, in front of the ridiculous eagerness of four valets dressed in black jackets, urgent and, so it would seem, ironic! It is quixotic! And yet their attitude of deep attention, their balletic step after each one of his gestures, finish by annoying him. Why are they looking at him like that? What is so strange about a confidential and extraordinary courier carrying sealed envelopes? In truth they were ridiculous these dummies with their rigidity of blind men suddenly springing into action with mad gestures simply because he needed a fork. Leave! Leave! Perhaps a cigar smoked on the river promenade will calm his agitation.

Oh! How autumnal is the evening river and how melancholic this slow passage of shadows as if they were exiled in Lachenfels; not a boat on the river, not a light opposite, nothing on the bank, life is dead; a few lights come out of the mists, infrequent lamp posts, reduced in number to preserve the romantic feel of the place. Only, in the distance, a few lights signal a military district lying at the foot of a monstrous fortress. Should he go there? What for; there will be neither light nor noise; it is just an illusion of distance. How tedious Lachenfels is; you could hear your soul rustling. Silhouettes of couples appear suddenly whilst others walk away in silence; voices of mystery, not of laughter; love is pale and white along the promenade beside the river, and this colourless river, just a burden in life, flowing slowly under this dark sky, in the night that had begun in a cloak of myth, opaqueness without constellations, the heavy weight of this town barren of lights, all this weighs heavily on good old Sparkling, court butterfly, walking aimlessly for once in his life beside the silence of the waters and of things.

More streets, the town is falling asleep. No doubt boredom caused by police decrees, but where are the inhabitants? For there are some, that is confirmed by the Baedeker guide. Sometimes lieder can be heard from afar, slow, drawling, the problems of weighty drinkers slowly expectorated. Sparkling is bored; and his footsteps take him back to the station where he had been wrong, bitterly wrong, to get off his train. Oh, further sadness, the long, empty platforms, misty, smoky with little oil lamps, long strategic platforms, routes to massacre, platforms to dispatch the cannon fodder of future battles. What is to be done, what can a man of taste and pleasure do here? The first train to arrive will be going to Krebsbourg; as far as his destination is concerned, no train before tomorrow morning and it is certain he will not sleep here; too bad if the train will take him back to Krebsbourg in a few hours, just at the time when in capital cities people are only just coming out of theatres. To immerse himself in joy once again, for a couple of hours in living life, to sleep; then he will set off on his mission again; but what is his mission? Doubtless some minor affair, for which one can certainly lose one day.

More sadness, the brutal, noisy languor of the train flying through the dense darkness, lights burned by speed, an unhealthy atmosphere. The speed of the train sems to brush against glass cages dotted around in a desert. At the ice-cold stops, vague souls, wrapped up, pale, impatient to set off again; small nightmares have turned these faces pale. There is something worrying about the night express which, from so far away, is carrying to the West crowds of foreigners speaking different languages;[1] it is the night express that transports the criminal and the sombre trickster. In the cor-

---

1 "Versilingue" in the text is a neologism. Our translation is based on "multilingue", someone who speaks a number of languages.

ner of the compartment where Sparkling has installed himself two men are smoking, dressed in too much black, with too many rings on their fingers, looking like Italian actors, shady businessmen, living suspects; women's names dropped in their conversations, with semi-irony hinting at low acts or petty crimes.[1] The large shape of a large bourgeois is dozing, an overbearing factory owner or a too-skilful trader.[2] Sometimes the Italians look at him strangely. A slight but acrid anguish keeps Sparkling awake; as the train runs along faces of employees steal a glance through the windows, a drab appearance, despite the little light from their lanterns, the pasty apparition and almost anguishing face of poverty or spying that had suddenly been revealed. This mission, what if it was a joke! Impossible to know, impossible to unseal the dispatches, but why this haste to see him leave this very day. Bah! A coincidence. However, if the King had played a joke, was it spurred on by his dear and yet so touchy and disagreeable to all, and especially to Sparkling, other inseparable minister, the Minister for the Civil List, he who comes to the palace in the morning and often, with his grumpy air brings to a swift end the happy conversation made joyously up of old jokes and anecdotes from the day before? The first hints of disgrace! That seemed strange this afternoon when this day was still bright; but at this sad and ambiguous hour the shapes of thoughts

---

1 This sentence contains two words "demi-ironies" and "ellipser" both of which are neologisms.
2 We have translated the French neologism "transacteur" as "trader".

are harsher and more hostile. We would see!! You do not knock Sparkling over by blowing on him; and then what would be the motives! The Queen having found out about the costly, libertine club, undermining him in the name of respectability, that was impossible to admit, yes, really, what a chimera; nothing to reproach himself for, nothing! Unless the King knows! . . . But how can one resist someone who says they love you, who says that Christian is difficult, annoying, that he is a fairy-tale, a tale that sends you to sleep, a fastidious element on an escutcheon, a very unfunny never hilarious conversation companion; the self-interest of the lady works against any revelation, and as far as discovering the truth, the King himself has never found out anything about his faithful Sparkling. So that was impossible, really impossible.

It was the customs post; at night, with ransacking gestures, the customs officers are a nuisance. Nothing is found, nothing is ever found; now it is the friendly faces of the Hummertanz customs officers who examine the cases; they have never found anything.

The wagons are rolling again in the thick darkness, across the flat fertile land. In the distance torches flame like tall furnaces. The passengers in the wagon are snoring moodily; what a bore! There must be some small festivity at the palace; no doubt there will be no one at home; if he went straight home and had the Duchess alerted she would be very surprised; she is at the palace festivity; for some time she has become strangely fond of going, in her finest dress, in all her beauty; ladies have these moments when they seem to come into flower again; she seems to have a more favourable view of the Minister for the Civil List . . . Ah! Decidedly this jitteriness is too stupid; it makes one have strange thoughts; what will come into his mind next? But this forced departure was very sudden, and doubtless for some petty affair, futilities that they all were busy with, he like the others.

Sparkling began to reflect deeply, anxiety made furrows in his brow and suddenly like a sleepwalker he cried out loud: "Blast it, that's why he is sending me on a mission!" The Italians and the dealer are woken with a start briefly then fall back to sleep. Sparkling opened a newspaper without reading, drew back the lampshade, put the paper down again, picked it up, looked at his watch. Soon they would be in Krebsbourg.

IV

DURING the day Krebsbourg is a capital that eats. From evening onwards Krebsbourg is a capital that snores.

At each and every ten o'clock in the evening there is a unanimous grinding of lowering shop fronts, of shutters being locked, of doors being luxuriously bolted. It is then that, in high, spacious and sparsely furnished bedrooms, the strong and calm middle class, the thrifty robustness of the country, falls asleep with big dreams of money to be earned, to be pampered and made fruitful. Tired from spending the whole day behind their counters weaving their spiders' webs to entrap passing écus,[1] Josephs and Josephines, Othons and Goths, Luitpolds and Marguerites are replenishing their strength in order, tomorrow, in fact every tomorrow, with the only break being the game of bowls on Sunday afternoon, to scratch out their existence again, fuelling themselves with heavy and comforting plate-

---

[1] Gold or silver coins current in the nineteenth century in many European countries.

fuls of vegetables. With their harsh, kitchen-garden brains, they snore in time and in tune, in the winding streets of the commercial district.

In the new districts, houses with inelegant and neat facades, slightly uncomfortable in line with the feudal rites of architecture, demonstrating by a few gold features on the balconies and highly wrought door knockers that their owners are high born, these protect the aristocracy. These descendants of the past have dozed off deploring the ultra-liberal way things are going, the tentacular perversities of an immoderate press, and the fact that the immoderate flow of atheisms is invading the universities. As with the bourgeoisie the same ample vegetable meals suffice, but set in old, metallic vessels. It is fashionable to savour infusions of chicory and weak teas in inconvenient and incandescent silver cups, over which are discussed trade unions, exploitation of mines, intensive farming, building of workers' cottages, which earn one or two per cent more than houses or commercial property; the discussion turns to the use of precious forecasts of the future, from the point of view of investment decisions, gleaned from conversations with highly placed people, close to the Church and its ministers. The Church of Hummertanz detests poverty; its basilicas are museums with ticket offices; wooden shutters hide its works of art and are only slightly opened by the chink of a coin; wooden cages, hermetically sealed, cover the mausoleums and the open sesame to these little doors is once again a coin. Only the fine, admirable stained-glass windows that project onto the white flagstones fans of mobile stonework have resisted the attempt to make people pay separately for the vision.

The Church is wealthy and strong. It has, so to speak, lay bankers and a mixed order of stockbrokers; its convents, well sheltered from foreign competition by a deep protectionism, produce beer, spirits, cloth and small ironmongery. Missionaries travel through foreign countries, not to evangelise, but to install vast hotels close to sites of natural beauty, where the exclusive view of earthly landscapes can be sold at eye-wateringly high prices. When the Government is in a spot of bother, trying to bring an architectural project to an end, the clergy comes to its assistance, lending it some old church or cloister to house its offices in exchange for a small reimbursement. The Church of Hummertanz is rich, even respected.

It is close to the spacious roads of the new town, near shady gardens, and the wide pavements of the aristocratic district that the narrow, silent, canonical streets begin, long pale-white convent walls; from rare windows, black-painted crosses on doors, above the walls there appear sparse, sickly treetops, and the evening is even quieter than in the business and aristocratic districts. Amongst these cenotaphs, vague staggering footsteps of a common man scarcely scratch the surface of the heavy silence of the opaque darkness.

Animation swirls about, pitiful and miserly, near the stations, around the solemn theatres, as though it were a holiday or a Sunday; it is tucked away in a few inns at one point on the boulevard, and quite capriciously frequented by a few foreigners reading newspapers in their own language; the heavy rattle of a coach is rare in these parts, and the lights of the pleasure spots are as if caulked and timid in the face of this reign of drabness and aridity. The laggards in these places seem to feel that criticism is weighing on them; censure descends from the porches and the bell-towers, spreads out from the banks with their model activity, falls from the equestrian and allegorical statues, from the brand new sphynxes of the Academic Palace, drizzles from the lodgings of annuitants and from workers' cottages; time is being wasted and so is money. The only ones with an excuse are the closed circles of the gentry[1] and of wealth; one can forgive the creators of massive halls that, used during the day as sales and auction rooms, and for wine trading, and that at night give shelter to activity on the wooden floor behind closed shutters, one can forgive them for disturbing those wretches who wish to sleep for a small charge. But those cafés on the Boulevard Mariahilf, frequented by foreigners, down and outs, bohemians and journalists, they were the small stain that disturbs Krebsbourg, in its stiff robe of solid virtue.

And it is here, near these relative lairs, that slowly, gently, languorously the Duke of Sparkling dawdles along, gnawing on scraps of thought and in a distressed mood, the Palace Marshal, Knight Commander of a large number of orders, a vivacious man, a happy man, a man moving in courtly and elegant circles, rich, well-connected, full of life (people never stopped telling him this), appreciated by High Society and by

---

1 In English in the original text.

the Church, despite his minor vices, respected by the bourgeoisie with an affectionate and respectful indulgence, this same Sparkling whose civilian elegance was appreciated by the Prince of Wales, whose military elegance eclipses by so much that of other attachés, during the summer manoeuvres that are one of the ornaments of the Empire of Niederwaldstein. He knew them a little these inns. A few youthful follies, a few foreigners taken there in accordance with the conventions of the Thousand and One Nights Club; clearly they did little more than pass through, to go to the galleries of the Stock Exchange where, in narrow streets, small establishments hinted that for a few pence, plus tips in proportion to the intentions one had, there were singers as scantily dressed as dancers.[1] But this evening Sparkling did not wish to adventure in; sometimes the official classes mistakenly took these places to be theatres, and so could be seen there, apart from slandering chancellery officers, Gouttegrass, the adipose chronicler, the cantata king of Hummertanz, who, having pivoted in the respectable salons where he alone could express aphorisms, flattering ones on Paul Bourget who had once written him a polite letter, or dismissive ones about many others who were pleased to be unaware of his existence, who had just run aground there for a few moments.

It was the little sliver of freedom allowed to literature; by his loyalty to the monarchy and his love of old

---

[1] Kahn's word "danseuses", literally "female dancers" is often used in French as a synonym of "mistresses".

customs, Gouttegrass was having his revenge; moreover Gouttegrass, rather despised for his profession, even though he did it very badly and made money out of it, was as talkative as a doorway, and with honeyed words traded all anecdotes that came into his servile possession. These small unpleasant acts forgave him, in his own eyes, for being the too humble guest of great palaces; moreover from them he drew a babbling and even a little childlike air which, he thought, made his very ripe age more attractive.

V

THE café where Sparkling stopped off was large, bright, creamy white, illuminated feebly by electric light reflected from gilded ornaments. Along the walls, in pale colours, a national painter had evoked the allegorical charms of countries that did not have the good fortune to be Hummertanz; Spain offered its mandolins, and the unbridled sinuous dance of a gipsy, red rose and mantilla. The Ottoman was smoking the hookah and his benign eyes were searching in the curves for a paradisiacal dream hinted at by a white and violet shape. Gnomes were pouring mead into the half-open mouths of sleeping peasants, this was Germany; the Tyrol was a male singer dressed in green close to a female singer dressed in pink.

But Switzerland was a moonlike blue mountain with a hotel at its peak; where England was concerned, the artist had painted people in check-patterned suits, leaving the quayside in a spritely manner to board a brand-new steamship. But what was the cause of their joy; were they leaving England or were they chartering it so as finally to return home? It was not very explicit.

Doubtless the painter had thought that it was better clearly not to upset Albion, so touchy and quick to take offence. To represent the good fortunes of France, a gentleman dressed in a frock coat, from the top of a stage, stretched an arm towards a not intentionally caricatural crowd; was it through a delicate attention to detail the apotheosis of our representative system or the liturgical representation of one of these moments of intense patriotic fervour sparked off, in cafés-concerts, by inspired patriotic songs? There could be some doubt about this; it was preferable to turn one's eyes towards pale and discordant tattoos that could easily represent either Italy or Japan. But was Hummertanz not present in this café of the Nations? Of course, it was! It was shimmering on the ceiling. A hefty goddess, an itinerant Juno, one hand resting on a peacock whose caudal feathers looked like large coins, was lowering the other towards the sovereign, stiff and buttoned up in black evening wear. A human-faced hydra was twisting powerless rage beneath its feet; its face was green and the tongue protruded from the left-hand side of its mouth, desperate claws shrivelled up vainly to grasp caskets and masses of paper, either a charter or some paper money. In one corner of the canvas workmen were raising their hats with tireless arms. The brilliance of Hummertanz could be seen on the metal adverts between the columns; the admirable and nutritious Hummertanz chocolate, authentic Hummertanz champagne, better and less expensive than the vintages from Epernay,[1] the insurance company against poverty

---

1 The centre for Champagne production in France with more

in Hummertanz, the only company in the world that paid out on all indemnities. Buffets were singing the praises of the porcine race of the country prepared in every conceivable way; as well as the marvels of salt fish whose factory may justifiably claim to be the supplier to the court and to the noblest foreign courts; the Fatherland shone in the jugs of beer on the tables, it sparkled in the conversation of the young people of Hummertanz, gathered there every evening. Although representing the most prominent tendencies towards opinions that undermine a throne and the happiness of a pacific coming together of citizens, they were the first to discover, in turns praising the national beer, that they thought they should frequently and even always celebrate the incontestable superiority over foreign ales because of its lightness, its aroma and its cheap price; there existed old fermented beers, sleeping the sleeps of years in the dry security of cellars, that one only opened with shaking hands; but at the very moment that they gathered together to conclude the evening with nectar, these young irregulars no longer vaunted the local liquid, they were all casting a slur on the exclusive growth of paper-money, in their graceless foster-mother of a homeland, and to remember the disgraceful acts of their official literary caste, of the followers, of the kneeling, bulging-cheeked, fat-lipped, solecizing, hypocritical, gang of that hated Gouttegrass; this was the inevitable peroration of the colloquium in the same way that the grateful invocation of their own Gambrinus was the exordium. And

---

than 100 km of underground cellars.

truly, these irregulars, the contrasting elite was correct for no country is like this country a drug and which could be found, beneath this low sky, through these flat streets, in order to make monotonous hours pass more quickly, by that rhetorical, satirical, oxymoronical, philotechnical, virtuosic, lyriformical tribe, except beer and tobacco. (Let us add that it was in no way through delicate attention in their case that the powers did not falsify this narcotic plant by an oppressive and tragic control; nor was it through generosity that they had not imposed hefty taxes on thirst for the bourgeoisie jealously defends its freedoms of the stomach and narcotics. If the State were thinking of monopolies in these areas, safes would close, and rifle shots would go off on their own.)

Sparkling was hearing, "Art dealers have set up businesses abroad with the sole aim of the exclusive exploitation of our aesthetic Mentors grouped into otherwise corruptible commissions.

"One of our compatriots, for purely mercantile reasons, recently set up a factory in Franconia, to provide our museums of archaeology with an inexhaustible supply of stone objects, of tapestries, of large drinking vessels and medieval furniture. The famous oak barrels, decorated with brass, the pride of our guildhall for all trade professions, were being embellished, encircled, ornamented by young workers for a World Exhibition, planned somewhere and which never came to fruition; nearly all the pictures in our museums have their counterparts in small galleries in Germany, and no one could really swear that we possessed the originals. Paris did not want our kakemonos[1] and treated them with the same disdain as that with which our bureaucracy rejected our contemporary painters of genius and talent who were dying of hunger in the hovels of bumpkins where life is poor. Our men of letters, the genuine, modern, archaic ones, have either sought rebuff abroad or were grafting themselves on to unworthy pen-pusherisms, whereas the Gouttegrasses, Wasserohts, Focarbecks, the court protégés imbibe the resources left to art through every pore, and suck them up with a display of things. Gouttegrass, for whom clerical and dowager duffers are benign, asks with a casual air and fills his purse, without counting, with an air of charming embarrassment. Wasseroht earns pensions and small profits for articles that measure our mental poverty, short articles to control the influx of foreign thought, and critical excursions in the guise of academic inspections. Focarbeck, the least important of these gentlemen, meagre foot soldier of serialised fiction, besieges the antechambers and gives the doorkeepers discounts on the subsidies he receives as bait, to obtain turns as someone seeking favour. That, Sir, is the state of affairs in our little country."

It was clearly a foreign man of letters they were putting in the picture; there followed a conversation in even lower voices. They chatted about things other than literature. Sparkling thought he heard his name mentioned; he could not make it out too clearly, but they were smiling; and indeed, was he sure that it was his name; moreover the anecdotes followed on one

---

1 Japanese wall art.

after the other. A man of letters, accused of trying to make money out of pornography, is hauled before a jury; in his defence he cites the country's liberal writers whose declarations are listened to distractedly; what is their entitlement and what is the authority of these fools. But the barrister has kept his last statement in reserve; he proves that the magistrates are purchasing at great cost the most characteristic products of the most clandestine review copies of books of a special circulation from the bookshop that paid the accused a few pence; and from this crack in the seriousness of the solemn council flows acquittal.

Another story: an unfortunate girl entered a convent, where for a few years, thanks to her ignorance and her simple mindedness, she is relegated to the lowliest of tasks. Suddenly her belly begins to get bigger, to inflate. This organ bulges, swells; it grows out, becomes gibbous; it is a breakwater, doubtless a leviathan. It terrifies, heavy and clumsy, ringing like a bell, the fresh innocent and candid downtrodden women besides whom, in this pious enclosure, the belly wobbles. Doctors are summoned, naturally doctors imbued above all with the sublime doctrines of the state religion. Consultation: the royal doctor evaluates the psalm writer, the apothecary exchanges views with the shit eater; will the piety of the holy women be revolted if the arcana of this shameful belly is closely examined: no, it is better to trust divine, etiological evidence; they judge the good woman to be pregnant. Strengthened by her obscure innocence she protests; rigorous tasks pile up on her; captivity and maltreatment, transfers to disciplinary convents, and science continues to predict that she will give birth. Finally and at length, with the full term of a normal parturition having elapsed, anxious about keeping in their midst what can only be the work of the devil, they throw her out penniless; yet the non-religious healers conclude in sufficient numbers that she has dropsy. The poor woman was outside any refuge, with no savings, and now only having as her sole hope the modest protection of the law, so favourable to true believers.

All of that was true! Sparkling knew about it in broad terms; except he had not really thought about it. Was what these young people were forecasting about the calm of Hummertanz, strikes, runs on the markets, violent opening up of the convents, the lay, brutal hands of the revolutionaries on the keys and on Peter's pence;[1] and the words spoken more softly, where he thought he had heard his name! It was no doubt similar prattling, but referring to personages, to conservatives. Official popularity was not without its down side; and the aristocratic disdain he had for the acclamatory crowd of burgomasters, aldermen, money changers that prevented him from hearing these statements with bitter displeasure showed him possible truths in what he was hearing, and also in what he could not perceive; he wanted to speak to them, to try by some means, to find out their opinions about the Duke of Sparkling, this was perhaps the way to end this ridiculous night; for he no longer wished to

---

1 A voluntary payment made since 1860 by Roman Catholics to the papal treasury.

go anywhere, neither to go home, nor anywhere else, to run after distressing certainties, even worse, to let himself become bogged down in these phantasms that had come into his brain because of the black of the night and by the nervous irritation of the railway; but how! How to broach the subject and tomorrow would he not be retaken by his sense of dignity, the incompatibility of social circles; Sparkling with his ironical passion for solemn chansonniers of sellers of nostrums, of the literary scribblers! And Sparkling to continue in his melancholy to soak up in his own way the glorious aboriginal chatter. Finally, despite his lassitude, the vague, tenacious and recurrent trance, a mechanical instinct induced him to stand up, not without having looked again with an almost friendly curiosity at these unrestrained young men, scarcely made notorious for him by some disdainful statements he had heard earlier; and doubtless from their point of view was he not an abusive chamberlain, a useless floral crown-wearer, such a vague marionette, and only by reputation, for not one of them seemed to have noticed him. The street lamps along the monotonous lines of stone, along the silent slopes were burning like expiatory hobgoblins; a funereal atmosphere hovered; the neo-byzantine architectures of the corpulent church buildings remained ghastly pale, sounding out thin and sad and too slow peals of bells. The streets, deserted apart from the lights rising from the basements of the houses; away in the distance, at some crossroads, the empty chatter of servants, looking at the passer-by as though he were a spy or a cut-throat, a shrill female cry, loud laughter at the doors of inns that were emptying, sleep-walking and haphazard watchmen, bowed down by the monotony of their task, then again the black, thick, dozy silence. Decidedly, nobody was having fun in Krebsbourg that evening, similar to all the evenings wasted by Sparkling. He was thinking about it; he might have arrived at a short, solid pessimism, if he had not been close to his house where, to his astonishment, several carriages were waiting.

However, it was not the illuminated luxury of evening receptions, nor the ostentation of livery. Having found out what was happening, Sparkling went towards a small salon, overlooking the gardens, one of the fantasies of the Duchess, a boudoir that had been sacrificed to this taste for knick-knacks which, coming from abroad, upset a little the internal rigidities of the Palaces of Krebsbourg, but only in a few, rare places; the King having said again and again that there would always be time to burden themselves with these trifles when national industry was capable of making them; that it was not worth opening a gaping wound in the country's flank, from which would flow the blood of savings. In this retreat the Duchess was holding an important congress of ladies. The idea that floated in the air at a few tea-parties, with tea and cakes, where this gracious elite gathered together in statements and satires, had suddenly, this very day, taken shape. In Africa, even in those colonies that the government had procured for trade, there were indubitably numerous bands of poor negroes; without doubt they had only two expectations about their future; either to be sold as slaves by the Arab merchants that impoverish the jobs of the colony that is our pride and joy by producing so many sober and cheap workers: or else, to squat beside their baobab trees in a ridiculous tranquillity, an ignorant belief in incomprehensible gods, rolling about naked in the grassland, diving into rivers full of hippopotamuses, distracting their contemplative hours with the shrill music produced by their gourds. His Highness the Primate of Hummertanz had already drawn attention to the exceptionally unfortunate case of this puny humanity; whereas the missionary restricted himself to accusing quietly and good-humouredly these victims of an ancestral fault, whilst gathering them together as closely as possible next to his establishments, assisted in this by a few detachments of troops, the explorer went further; the child-like people were, in his opinion, perfidious, secretive, miserly. Caring so little for any morality or administration, the native used the ruses of a black man to hide his stock of riches. Any means were good, so as not to exchange goods with the tutelary and paternal European; one had even seen them reject brandy, turn down fine, brand-new rifles, fashioned for them by friends of the State and costing three or four francs to manufacture, adequate arms except that, in their own interests, every subterfuge was invoked not to complete this sale through the addition of a few cartridges. These clear proofs of barbary, advanced without challenge other than very minor differences of perspective by the only authorised voices of Hummertanz, the priest and the trade explorer, had touched the hearts of these ladies.

It was a question of working, in a connected way, by means of the two forms of influence previously cited, on the civilisation of or even, if that were possible, the taming of the negro: the adult negro had to be calmed and groomed, the negress dressed (for on this point all had not been said but much had been left to be guessed at), the pampered negro children, and a few of the most select specimens of the race, chosen in infancy, imported into the great ports of Hummertanz. Their education, entrusted to worthy priests, would permit them to be trained for the special service of their benefactors, of their patrons, of their sovereigns, or rather of the retinue of their sovereigns, of their sovereign landholders. It was an obvious strategy. Not without jealousy Europe would applaud this profiting from colonisation, one of the most useful of its type; all the more so since the white man, even the one drawn towards humility by good religious and monarchic doctrines, was beginning, as was the white woman, to be less and less obedient, the servant, the person of confidence dreamed of by aristocracies and bourgeoisies. All these ladies were only too aware of this, even more than aware, and it was the mutual communication of these certainties that had prolonged the evening, that was still prolonging it, the elegant synod only having had a few brief minutes during these hours to get dear utopia ready and implant it in the order of facts.

Sparkling congratulated them on allying their grace to their strength, in view of a more floral expansion of the political programme of the King. He was almost happy, his fears subsided; had it not been for the slight worry about finding in the membership of the planning committee the wives of the Minister for the Civil List and of the Railway Minister, both of whom detested him with all their extra-maturity, their false piety and their ambition, he would have been blissful. If the Duchess is whitening the souls of negroes through raffles, small theatrical shows, whilst far away hiring, she and other young women, desperate philanderers, and is reducing a few special economies for the better of the general interest, for the partial interest of two fractions of the continent, then so much the better. Moreover, at that moment, he would have greeted with pleasure any captivating (and time-filling) activity that might have soothed this rather vague and empty soul, this elegant person, of false dreams, of unoccupied practical bent that was the Duchess.

The tragic hypotheses, so painful, the self-doubt and doubt of others, the tenacious and cruel trance faded away; he had a few moments of joy, and the playful lord regained all his variegated colours, his flags of gaiety in good company, his joyful instincts in lesser company; clearly these two Parcae[1] who were smiling at him in a prickly way, with honeyed voices would talk of his presence if that could do him harm; but were the ladies aware? The Duchess of Sparkling, altruistic, humanitarian! What a wonderful thing! All that worry about fashion from Vienna obliterated by the horizon of Wilhelmina-City,[2] with chapel, cloakroom, processions of negroes, etc., in the imposing

---

1 Fates.
2 "Wilhelmina-City" in the original text.

houses, in schoolrooms, pictures with inscriptions, gift of the Duchess Wilhelmina Sparkling, née Hohenfall, as she called herself on her brief public appearances to indicate to what degree her dear Duke ennobled her, but also what her own profile was without him; she would reign over the distribution of gifts with charming and becoming gravity; this Wilhelmina-City becoming from the first branch, from the second brick, thanks to the official State geographers, the last word in civil planning. In what apparel would the faithful subjects be dressed, no doubt with the best possible taste. Perhaps a general outfit, half-livery, half-military uniform for the men, and no doubt, by contrast, for the women a muddle of striking colours, of course those that go well with a tint of ebony. A delicate question; yellows and reds, no blue or green, and definitely no purple! Would they be lace-makers? The hair style of the inevitable cigar-makers would need to be organised; and the first products of domestication! But no need to bother about that, between now and then she would have other worries! And Sparkling, listening to the pitter-patter of the words, sketched out in his mind the district, with its workshop of little chimera, peopled with thoughtful ladies of easy virtue, that the Duchess was building alongside that gravelled, well-emblazoned, so London-park-like city where normally she paraded her soul in a noble carriage pulled by four horses, with white livery and silver buttons. The two Parcae no doubt saw no more in this than a means of enjoying exotic desserts at a cheaper price, as did other ladies! There were two of them, the wife of a referendary courtier, and the wife of a senator ship-owner, both of them quite pretty, and the Duke could not calculate their future progress in the field of colonial charity without a secret jollity.

And so it was, very happy, fit and well, that he withdrew, vaguely referring to duties, political tasks, to leave the salon and the house and to head towards pleasure, the particular pleasure that he had arranged for himself in a discreet garden square, not very far away in the city. It is true that the Duchess had seemed surprised by his arrival, pulled away from her pleasures, very indifferent about his departure; the blue of her eyes had sometimes become deeper as she looked at her husband; but enough of that! All that with the nightmares of the journey, crack-brained notions, dreams like bubbles of bad air. Everything was fine, if the King was not visiting Nelly Albestern, statuesque opera singer, as white as Hebe, as blonde as Aphrodite, as coarse in language and gesture as a Paris street urchin. The King had singled out Nelly. Nelly had singled out the faithful Sparkling, a devil who was stirring in a different way from his sovereign. She could not single out anyone else; it was her duty to respond to royal taste; this the Duke realised not only as a faithful vassal but as a man of the world who knew that, in the case of a break-down in the relationship with the King, the actress's continued presence in the capital would become difficult for her.

Christian had shown himself harsh in similar circumstances. Then, in high society, should pleasure not be enhanced by epicureanism and attractive nonchalance. All the same, this duality completed the royal physiognomy and confirmed in him what political exiles called his good side, despite the severity of his hierarchical portraits, and the gift that loyalist sculpture made of his two profiles, the right-hand side belonging to the Hohenzollerns and the left to the Hapsburgs; it was while thinking these disrespectful thoughts that suddenly, at the corner of a street, the joyful walker found himself face-to-face with his august master, returning alone and on foot, and escorted only very vaguely and at a distance.

The Duke was discomfited; the King, irritated, started with some general remarks about the surprising nature of the encounter and the lovely beauty of the night. Moving on to present circumstances, he congratulated himself that the Duke was in good health, not without being astonished that it should be precisely in Krebsbourg, at the intersection of the Lowenstrasse and the Tonstrasse, a place eminently appropriate to be trodden by the footstep of a Palace Marshal, but not at the very minutes when the latter was accredited as an ambassador to some favourite and monarchical cousin that this meeting should take place. It was hard to believe that the Palace Marshal, the Duke of Sparkling, added to his incontestable aptitudes the gift of ubiquity: also, to attribute the unexpected presence of the Duke to a phenomenon of magical wizardry would have been audacious, for there are no wizards in Hummertanz, even in its ministries, and nothing permits the claim that they are to be found in any of the neighbouring states, even Niederwaldstein. It was useless to convince himself that his special orders, although revered and loved by dear old Sparkling, possess such special means of transport, even though they were so light to carry, to be brought back in such a brief period of time. Doubtless the Marshal did not have a bluebird as in fairy stories; he could not have entrusted his telegrams to a providential passing carrier pigeon. As far as using a special train was concerned, King Christian knew that was totally impossible in the light of the private documents he received about the management of his railways. In any case, he would be delighted, in place of a reply to his telegram that he could not hope for, to obtain from the Duke a snatch of short explanatory truth.

Saying this, from the colossal height of his body, his eyes widening as far as possible in his face well-worn although surrounded by admirable white curls, King Christian looked down on his companion, without kindness.

It was because of an urgent dispatch, received not far from Krebsbourg when the train had stopped briefly, an instantaneous dispatch sent by the Duchess so that he could be present expressly this very evening, even very late at a secret meeting about an interesting project close to the royal aims in the matter of lofty civilisation and colonisation, that Sparkling excused his presence; very soon, in the morning, he would set off again. He hoped that he had succeeded in the choice of his zeal, between two ways of serving him who sometimes deigned to regard him as a friend, having been able to give the Duchess the advice that she needed, and that the mission would be accomplished with minimal delay; besides, if the King did not require his company, which was futile given this clear evening and with the streets of the faithful city without danger, he intended to return home so as to set off again on his mission as early as possible.

Could it have been the sudden evocation of the Duchess (Sparkling was irritated by that), could it have been that Sparkling had just rendered service to the Civil List in its dear possessional form, there was a recovering of equanimity, and with three or more different modulations, the following words came forth:

"My dear Duke, the object of the mission was not urgent; I want even to tell you that it was pointless; but you are aware, in our milieu, even amongst people closely linked to business, that you are sometimes criticised; not that one thinks of tarnishing your friendship, fidelity or devotion; but people think you are frivolous; brilliant but frivolous; I would have liked to make clear that your speed of movement was without reproach. Europe, my dear Duke, is going through a crisis, or rather the symptoms of a very hidden crisis are becoming apparent. These are signs of the times; you do not see them, you whose service is above all rendered by the appropriate pomp, brilliant décors, and high courtesy in which you excel; I know that the charm of your relations, your conversation, that your good humour is not without influence over our illustrious friends and their well-intentioned diplomats; but nevertheless the present hour demands that the men of Hummertanz are serious, very serious; the

Minister for the Civil List to whom today I was explaining this opinion would back it up with precious and instant insights. Revolution is rumbling, my dear Sparkling; will it be economic, political, social as they say with a new word, I do not know, I cannot say; perhaps it will be all those things at once: in any case, I can say that if a political crisis is rather useful to us since Hummertanz, protected from wars, is benefiting at the moment from its calm to shelter rich foreigners fleeing the theatre of war (there is here a question of taxation to be studied, my dear friend) an economic crisis would be of an incontestable seriousness for us. We have nothing, nothing to gain from an economic crisis; when he heard me say this, it was confirmed, evidence to hand, by the Minister for the Civil List."

Decidedly Sparkling's rival, the odious Minister, had the wind in his sails. How could he be combatted; he must have used base flattery! The King was parroting him word for word.

"And in these hard times, dear Marshal," continued the ominous voice, "all men of goodwill must gather round the throne with conscientiousness: on all sides our neighbours are encumbering us with evil-thinking exiles, whose ardours we are doubtless calming, whom we are sometimes expelling, but whose influence can be contagious, the very stability in our major cities perilous. God forbid that I should challenge the admirable spirit of order of our populations, but danger is finally rumbling around us. We must, dear Marshal, defend true liberties with energy, and I say it again, with seriousness. Let us not be like that Greek;[1] let us not put serious affairs off until tomorrow. Pleasures may come later. Now let us reign, rule and be ready."

These were the very words of the overweening rival; he was definitely the provenance of the Greek; the Duke was enraged, but even the influence of the hated Minister could not at this point have pushed the King in a taciturn direction; and so, Sparkling inquisitively asked about how Madame Nelly Albestern was at that moment.

"Ah! Dear friend!" (the point had struck home), "I can tell you since you are not only a Minister but a friend, I am tired of Madame Albestern. Can you imagine, and I really do not know who can be putting these weird ideas into her head, a head that I thought very sensible (you must have also sometimes noticed, Sparkling, that her judgment was good), well, these qualities have taken a wrong turn; she complains, pretends to fear being abandoned in the future, she is jealous of me; she has even told me that she wanted to be a countess, yes, a title of countess, with some vague settlement, for posterity's sake; do you think, my dear friend, that I could behave like that? But where can she be getting this idea; no doubt my cousin in Hummerkopf has this ridiculous mania for ennobling people, but I cannot do that, she would be better off giving up the idea." Sparkling was tempted to indicate, with subtlety, that such a clear care for reputation could only emanate from the treacherous advice of the

---

[1] Possibly a reference to Aergia, goddess of procrastination, although the Greek in Kahn's text is male.

most sadly positive man in the country, the Minister whose only knowledge of the world was finance, and who detested by his very nature truly sincere characters like Sparkling. And openly, with gaiety, he might have asked if the sovereign had not just let slip, in his presence, some dangerous or at least inopportune confidence. If this was so he had the chap in his power; but such short meditation was cut off. "I cannot see any good coming from this, these irritations are annoying me, and it is because I am avoiding them that you see me at this hour on foot in the street: I have left the place; but since you are there, you are going to make her see sense. She listens to you; your likeable and lively although solid personality, I am pleased to recognise, appeals to her; you have a good influence on her; put her at my service, my dear friend, let us go straight away, I only left her an hour ago; your pleasant intervention will dissipate this bad feeling; you will bring this minor foolish pretention to an end. Come, my dear friend."

In no way was the excellent friend pleased. He raised objections about the timing and the unexpected nature of the visit.

"But this evening," replied the King, "I too was unexpected; it is of no consequence that in this house I am unexpected. So, come my dear friend." They went there chatting: the King serious, Sparkling half defeated, half content.

The first impression was painful; a loud noise was raising the roof in the basement of the building, they waited, they saw quite distinctly though the windows a huge party in the kitchen; clearly champagne was popping; there were ladies-in-waiting, and nonchalant cigars in fat joyful lips. When someone came, it was with an unsteady step. On the staircase where the noise of footsteps was deadened by animal skins, a lady-in-waiting who had leaned over as though worried, the principal lady-in-waiting, rushed to meet them; Madame was resting, she was unwell; the King frowned; that people were drinking, having a good time downstairs as soon as he had left, was of doubtful majesty, but after all Madame may have been unaware of it; but that faithful Betty should attempt to block his path, with such a pretext, with a timid and anxious air, tearful but with what precise pretext? Open-mouthed he looked at Sparkling who was afraid to understand and they were both pushing the servant aside when there was something like a brief sound of struggle, two explosions, the door to the landing violently opened, and the second son of the King, Prince Max-Eric, wounded and bleeding, rolled into the arms of Sparkling, whilst a man's face, briefly seen on the landing, was disappearing and when a frightened and clumsy escape could be heard through the breaking of objects and distraught cries of a woman in distress. Sparkling had carried the young man towards the bedrooms: like a sleepwalker the King was following him, his jealous anger dissipated, too dissipated; with the Prince placed on a divan, they ought to have pursued the murderer, but through a wide-open window, looking over a garden linking up with a whole series of gardens, could be seen a silhouette appearing on a wall jumping down and then reappear on top of another one.

Moreover Sparkling had recognised him, and to the questioning of the King, who without looking at her was letting Madame Albestern curl up in hysterics, he replied: "I recognised him, I have no doubt about it, it is Golzer, the comic actor of the Theatre Royal."

And the King said: "What a business," and took his head in his hands. Fat tears rolled down onto his snowy-white beard.

AN INVIGORATING LONG JOURNEY

I

A few brief weeks had gone sadly by since the body of Prince Max-Eric, snatched away from popular affection by a devastating pleurisy (this was diagnosed and confirmed by two doctors from his regiment and by two learned faculty professors), had departed, in sombre luxury and with plaintive music, towards the small antique church sheltered by the blackish green of a forest-like park, not far from the capital. From the palace to the church, along the pavements, the bourgeois guard[1] was drawn up opposite the royal guard and both were presenting arms to the wide catafalque overburdened with crowns, to the warhorse limping (traditionally) beneath an entanglement of crêpe, to the envoys of different foreign powers, white-haired representative military men with their bemedaled decked-out chests, with shimmering materials, trios of young princes with the popular appearance of simple lieutenants. King Christian had followed the cortege on foot to the cathedral church with the marvel of its

---

1 Kahn will explain later (in Chapter III of *Perpetual Erynnies*) what is meant by "bourgeois guard".

stained-glass windows, based on the central panel of a famous triptych by Dürer of which the outer panels had formerly been sold in Hesse and in Saxony. His ear, distracted and heart-broken, had taken in as a vague buzzing the Bossuet-like[1] words of the worthy Cardinal Primate; the enthusiasm of the special crown musicians had impacted upon his eardrum without engraving their accents on it. After the blessings said at the placing in the tomb, the catafalque had swayed heavily then set off again. On the vast square, in the middle of the military cordon, humble people, women in mystical funeral veils and monkish bonnets, had prayed and wept, the round tears running down their whiteish, anaemic faces, genuinely moved by the premature nature of this death, and gripped, violated by the festive and lugubrious structure of the ceremony. Close to them were mixed orders of people; congregations of catholic workers assemble their genuflecting baldness around stiff banners with gold threads whose bearers were trying to reconcile a rather military and upright pace with the gentle stooping of someone drooping with sadness. A few had pretended to throw themselves in grief beneath the horses' hooves, a simple gesture emanating from a very ancient ritual.

Then coming back to the streets and their overflowing straight lines of troops, there had disappeared behind the cortege the King on foot, then the war horse, with outstretched arms the bearers of decorations displayed on cushions, the representatives of foreign

---

1 Bossuet was a seventeenth-century French theologian, noted for his sermons particularly at funerals.

powers, the unions of official bodies, the pious groups that had recently been at prayer, the synods of dissidents, the columns of devout women in lamentation, the delegations from the church factories giving rise to the presence at this sad procession of representations in painted and gilded plaster of the god and saints of the State Religion; bishops were praying beneath canopies of mourning, whilst the rhythm was set by elegiac brass instruments. Then between the ranks of cavalry, the court carriages, with their horses led by the hand by lackeys, the horses darkened by a band of crêpe going from their necks to their heels, and then troops, troops, with arms reversed, then silent gun batteries, and more cavalry. The slow procession was passing by, beneath balconies and windows, overloaded, expensively rented by the curious onlookers gathered together; then Prince Max-Eric was laid to rest in the little church, to sleep there for ever and to have his familiar dream about military manoeuvres and love affairs.

The Queen exiled herself for months, in a far-off castle close to heathland and opaque lakes where no boat ventured, made darker on the horizon by black pine trees like cypresses in the distance, for a long time empty and without guests, untouched by the pompous frivolities of the court; Christian never graced it with even the shadow of his presence. She only took a few close friends, among them the Duchess of Sparkling, whose grief was touching and exquisite, all ivory-like and mauve, her magnificent and multiflorous blonde hair, narrow, pulled tight, until it only looked beneath her veils like a plaque of ancient gold, barely noticeable, and the good old librarian Thaler, whose long speeches flow abundantly, correct and gentle during the invincible sleeps beneath the lamp, so short-sighted and polite that he apologises to the chair where he is meant to sit for having bumped into it slightly, mistaking it for one of his considerable gentleman or lady benefactors, and the inseparable chaplain to whom the Queen talks, without ever listening to his responses of courtly orthodoxy, modulated always into a spiritual and semi-ardent song of praise to the Virgin.

Christian returned to his palace and found out to his satisfaction that very few arrests had been necessary to maintain order on this day of bitter solemnity; rapidly he initiated the heir presumptive into state secrets that he and his ministers still possessed. During the following days he vegetated, taciturn and unapproachable, and announced to his Palace Marshal that with court mourning having been decreed, and through a sub-order the necessary recommendations having been carefully made, there were a few countries of his own choosing, both near and far, that the Duke could visit; in any case and at any time, his presence in Hummertanz would be judged less important than the future topics of conversation with his sovereign that he was bound to accumulate during a long trip abroad. The fluid skill of Gouttegrass convinced the press of all political opinions to accept the official story pronounced from the very top about the death of Prince Max-Eric; only the director of the *Fait Accompli*, Grossings, who doubted, doubted for a few days, without however advancing any precise argument, just simple objections, necessitated a few visits from this chamberlain of letters. His last visit persuaded Mr. Grossings, who was notoriously short of money, to publish with touching footnotes a few schoolboy exercises of Prince Max-Eric. At the same time, he stopped going to see Madame Albestern, for he was sometimes making her life gloomy. This lady suddenly found herself obliged to carry out engagements far away and to lavish her voice and her beauty in cities where Mr. Golzer was continuing his dramatic career, but in a different style and gathering laurels principally in honourable classical tragedy. All of that was without any possible correlation with royal and national mourning. Sparkling was bestriding Italy; ostensibly he was yawning amongst masterpieces; he visited versatile scientists, cultivated diplomats with an acumen moreover without contemporary use. He rendered service to, or accepted the respects to him from, the branches of the noble Hummertanz families that could be seen in this country. Not a single important Hummertanz family that did not have its representative in Rome, to live there through similitude, wholly closer to the Pope. He frequented Germans bogged down with notes in the margin, with lily-like features, and Britons, specimens of an ancient art abolished in this too frivolous Italy, totally disillusioned French psychologists. He saw without looking, looked without being seen. Perhaps it is true that, at certain moments, birrerias[1] were blessed and favourite, and that some-

---

1 Italian beer cafés. Kahn misspells the word as "birerias" in the text.

times he wandered astray around cities in the twilight; but the moment of the setting sun, bar of splendour in the mediocre day, is favourable to the reflexions of statesmen who are plotting the Atlandides[1] of a future triumph, the result of the force of combinations conceived in the age of experience. The Duke, joyful, gave himself touches of profundity, and in the manner of Socrates engaged willingly in conversation with beautiful ladies passing by, continuing to live his dream of beautiful women. No doubt the harmonious cadence of a ballet involves the whole harmony of movement, and its grace, and its multiple allegories; and further, the vision of a ballet magnifies, if one puts aside opera glasses, as too modern an instrument, the beauty of the women chosen to play the role, in style, of the eternal Eve. Sparkling told himself all this as frequently as possible and kept tight control of the distances that extend their irrepressible images between the vision of the whole and the complete excursions of detail. It is not established beyond doubt that one evening Sparkling composed a sonnet, in the style of New Life, that is to say apparently passionate about a lady who turns out to be, when you boil it down, no more than a vibrant eucharistic idea.

    King Christian remained morose; instead of annoying his courtiers with meddlesome little jokes, he avoided them. The opening of the Chambers, the secular sermons, not without a few bizarre rhetorical flourishes on the increasing solidity of Hummertanz, the demonstrations about hunger, nothing cheered

---

[1] Daughters of Atlas.

him up. He only broke his taciturn silence to grumble that certain delegates of his power would be more usefully employed in raking the earth in places he knew well, or in reclaiming land for agriculture in the new colonies, rather than complicating with their stupidities the march of events in Europe, insofar as for a tiny part their unfortunate existence could make any contribution. He treated like a dog the colonel of the bourgeois guard who had come to ask him innocently to review a fancy march past, asked the Minister for Agriculture whether he was even capable of milking a cow and declared pointedly to a friend in favour of the abolition of the land-tax body, that the authors of the constitution of Hummertanz had deceived the goodwill of his venerated father with crass stupidity, that he had unintelligent ministerial henchmen and whose fault was it, "the land-tax body only sending him jackasses and the universities and the state schools only young wild boars". The Minister for the Civil List begged him to avoid an appalling scandal; he threw him out swearing that it was a good job, and yet it was serious. There you are.

One of the colonial companies founded with special rights granted by the King, who was also incidentally the main shareholder, had held a conference in Geldwachs, the country's most important port. The debate was about inculcating into the dependency the industrial ardour of the home country and about asking in exchange for more profitability. The men of money had, to this purpose, summoned the men of science to debate with them in the splendid house by the canals, so famous for its semi-hieratical, semi-modern décor, obtained by the application of immense filing cabinets in pitch pine to the magnificent mouldings of light, locking in the emerald green of pigeon-holes, against walls decorated with old and majestic Spanish leather, with gold floral designs and reflected dark crimson. The result of the speeches, toasts, enquiries and balance sheets was that a mission chosen among the maturing and juvenile elite of Geldwachs should leave, to set off for there, to explore the plains, search in the forests, travel up the rivers, and everywhere to found something, in whatever model best pleased them, but to found always and everywhere whatever might increase the supply of ivory and bring in supplies of groundnuts. On the evening of this decision the mature elite gathered in the salons of notorious ship owners, and the juvenile elite paraded in pomp around the immense docks area of Geldwachs; this selection of young men drank German beers to its better future in huge white brasseries, where Tyrolians continually affirm their homesickness,[1] drank foaming stouts in metal tankards in cafés gleaming red with nickel and coloured glass, where English sea captains, worthy and roguish, looked on with contempt at the talkative, gesticulating drunkenness of their American colleagues. They made wishes for themselves in pubs where can be found the best gin for export, and the most supreme tafia rums for import; the whole was crowned by a copious common meal eaten in a great cosmopolitan hall, where

---

1 Kahn uses the German word "Heimweh" in the original.

English, German and French singers came one by one to give their audience the most unfavourable idea of their mother country, and concluded their exchange of views on their respective good fortune where extra-European expansion was concerned, through a judicious choice of the best wines, sparkling or not. At this new conference, different from the daytime one, were summoned Burgundies and Champagnes, the driest Rhine wines, and even Asti, so much so that there was no one at dawn amongst these apostles who did not see himself, depending on his temperament, as a Christopher Columbus, a Stanley or simply a Balboa.[1]

The ship that carried them away, a comfortable white-painted steamer, sounded its siren with a bellow for a short time, in the middle of the flag-bedecked ships and small yachts that accompanied them with their tender acclamations; the great steamship, still that same day, illuminated the sea with scintillating outbursts of happiness, glass in hand. It took them without incident to the ports of Africa, to the new Jerusalem of the explorable Canaan. Then soon one learned that they had chartered a flotilla of small boats, that the scientists and the adventurers were sailing on the main river, with native soldiers, austerely dedicated to the good of the generous home country. Then nothing more was heard. More than a year later, through an expedition of a thousand men armed with rifles sent to find out what had happened and who happily triumphed over a few tribes armed with arrows

---

[1] Vasco *Núñez* de Balboa, a 15th-16th century Spanish explorer.

and clubs, one learned that they had been eaten. Sad relics of their sufferings and their enthusiasm were announced to the stricken families of Geldwachs, where mourning appeared, darkening the foreheads, the costumes and the happy and silvery appearances of existence. It was just then, when projects for monuments had been conceived, that prose and official verse had been moved cacophonously, that an opposition newspaper threw a sort of fire-cracker, letters and diaries of memories it had received from the relative of one of the humblest members of the mission, a man it had taken on with the rank of a cook. The most distressing revelations about morals rapidly made dissolute and purely local, that the missionaries immediately and in their entirety and willingly adopted, burst forth each day with the precision of fireworks. The finishing pieces followed the Roman candles; it was nothing but wheeling and dealing of slaves, exchange of negresses, pillage of native property, proofs of a friendship with the State that went as far as to borrow from it without counting; in the case of the serious and learned people, burdened to breaking point by responsibilities, in the case of the mature rather than young men, it was a miraculous flourishing of the vice of primitive clans with a truly charming abandonment and the most childlike grace; the inconsolable women who walked, sadly and dreamily, along the melancholic jetties, looking at the sea on which he left and on which he will return, learned with fury that they had been purely and simply duped; the details transmitted not with cynicism but with an exquisite simplicity by the good cook tortured their hearts every day, all the more so since this gallant man held nothing back, and told the stories of them all, with the active zeal of someone who wants to put another totally in the picture. One could not put forward that it was the work of the opposition; it was private letters and diaries of memories that were being published, and the pure glory of the disappeared was tarnished by it, especially at Geldwachs where pietism is only effaced by rapacity that together compose the depths of soul of a ship owner of the noble city. Yet, this publication could have been avoided; the Director of the *Fait Accompli* had foreshadowed his power; a few sums of money, a few honours would have deterred this excellent fellow from casting this formidable scandal to the winds. Christian did not even wish to see him nor to give authority that he might in the future receive a reward for his silence. His only role in the affair was to ask the Minister for Railways what special textbooks of elegant life he allowed into the country and consented in jest to endow Geldwachs with a quite adventurous elite; the functionary mumbled, blushing, that he was sure of his railway wagons, but that since Geldwachs was a seaport the responsibility had to fall, he was very sorry to say, on his colleague from the navy; at this the sovereign replied that the most right-minded inhabitants of the town of Geldwachs seemed to him to possess the souls of commercial travellers; the city was very saddened by this and vowed to itself not to re-elect the mayor, during whose mandate such an insult should fall from the most authoritative of mouths.

The genuine irritation of the King, his annoyance at finding himself bound hand and foot by the mourning in his palace, his despair at only seeing turned towards him faces that were obsequiously grieving and commemorative of the recent misfortune, these all led him to think seriously about a plan for an escapade. To go away, to leave everything in the care of his ministers! Since their job was to expedite business, let them expedite it, he himself would go and spend a few days as a tourist; he would taste a joy of holidays, he would be somewhere, his hands in his pockets like a stroller, he would read a foreign newspaper, and news articles that did not interest him. But he needed a companion; the companion for escapades was in essence his dear friend, the good old Duke.

Sparkling had benefited from his absence; in the King's dreams he was once again chivalrous and joyful, quite close to his own sense of humour, even worthy of affection; is it necessary in order to amuse and distract a travel companion to be so capable of major governmental hard work. And so, our good friend the Duke received a hand-written letter fixing a rendezvous at Pohlstock, he was to travel incognito and would find at the terminus not the King, but his perfect effigy, Count Muller; no doubt he could for a few days agreeably go under the name of Baron Schulze, and discretion and precision were asked of him.

Pohlstock, the ancient capital of a minor margraviate, annexed since 1815 by the voracious Niederwaldstein, in an irreproachably flat plain extends the calm of its wide, abundant roads, bordered by open gardens,[1] accumulating fat roses and dahlias in the direction of the entrances to little cottages of a Dutch taste; a few of these light, small buildings offer reminiscences of pagodas such as may be seen on painted plates; some have evocations of the low Rhineland houses, with wide roofs, bulging with very neat woodwork; honest and familial mottoes beribbon themselves in polychromies intended to be graceful. Ironworks, carefully wrought, sometimes a happy decoration of earthenware nameplates arrest one's eye. Through a caprice of the founder of the town, Margrave Joachim Egbert, an offshoot of the Hohenglanz branch, the roads of the town fan out from a fairly large palace, a chalky, square building; what about the décor of the facade? A black and white frieze on which can be seen Arminius[2] on horseback, followed in Indian file by the successive incarnations of the heroes of Teutonia, helmeted, armour-plated, encased in iron, followed a little more comfortably dressed by elegant Rhinegrave ladies, and ending with the modest uniform of the grenadiers of the margraviate, a short time before this bellicose little country fell into the considerable bosom of Niederwaldstein; in the interior the State had paternally installed a guard house, and a few offices, amongst them the secret office of the commissioner of police. On the square, between four baskets of rhodo-

---

1 We have translated "jardins à claire-voix" in the original text as a misprint for "jardins à claire-voie".
2 Arminius, chieftain of the Germanic Cherusci tribe, who commanded an army in 9 AD that destroyed three Roman legions.

dendrons, a chrome Joachim Egbert was rearing up, an ingot of copper before the horizon, gentle, and yet majestic, and his yellow hand holding, dictatorially, a scroll of the same colour. It was a commander's baton, or a rolled-up legal document, or a manuscript, only practical jokers might have taken it to be a sausage.

As you walked along any of Pohlstock's streets you quickly came to the immense park that completely drowned it in its meanders, spacious walks, interrupted by small lakes with swans, and reflected its weeping willows in the attractive course of the Zehl, pretext for comic-opera windmills, red and white bricks, green shutters and which are on feast days taverns rather than serious flour mills.

In one of the most neatly cultivated parts of the park there stretches the ground floor of a small house called the Favourite, surmounted by an attic, and close to other small houses; it was there that, as he became older, Joachim Egbert had almost shut himself off from the world, with a few old close friends, only visiting the official palace for a few duties, anxious to escape from it again as quickly as possible and to allow the Margrave not to reign at all, but to write, this woman having been one of the greatest letter writers of the eighteenth century, a proven dissertator and philosopher consulted by all the intellectuals of Niederwaldstein with whom she exchanged idle talk, remunerating them a little. Tired of being present at this apostolate, Joachim Egbert had had built to his own taste his private chapel, had had it constructed according to his designs, and decorated in his image, the true image, as different as possible from the fine Roman whose effigy enriched the main square, turning his back on the detested palace. It was towards this architectural fantasy and its attached museum, a little faded with time, that in good humour our two wanderers headed; for the story of the old recluse had often assailed the ears of King Christian; for his father had often predicted to him, in his infancy, during his best years of inattention to affairs, that to despise the serious business of ruling makes even the naturally best prepared child, weak of intellect and likely to finish his days morose and manic, given over to inexplicable dissipations like this madman Joachim Egbert, the only madman in the static and cerebrally stable race of Hohenglanz. In the face of this reprobate memory an underlining of the great corresponding European glory completed the lesson so that Christian kept a joyous memory of this ancestor like a bogey man; what this special madness that threatened him was, he had no idea, neither had his worthy father; a few books could perhaps have enlightened them, but they never read; besides it would have been no more than gossip for in the dynasty one kept silent about the details of the life of the compromising and annoyingly exceptional ancestor, he was talked about quietly, with hints, as if one feared arousing in her hypogeum[1] the soul and the pen of the excellent lady writer afflicted by him.

The incognito of the great men of this earth is so difficult to maintain (what could be responsible for

---

1 Underground tomb.

that, their serene beauty or the radiant efflorescence of international police forces), that beneath the peristyle decorated with slender columns of granite-like marble, Doctor Vana, an aulic[1] councillor, curator of the monument, was respectfully presented to them by the very high born Major Baron von Langhirsch, sent by his sovereign in haste to do this and also to send them his greetings and to hand to them an august missive, being truly sorry not to have known in time to come and be of service to them in their hotel. The Major, whose walk irresistibly evoked the idea of a stork, was extolling to them the erudition of Doctor Vana, particularly useful that day, whose bearing meticulously evoked the fantasies of an earthenware jar.

The small doctor implored the noblemen to please put on the obligatory dress for visiting imperial castles, broad grey felt slippers that bore witness to the skill of those that the judicial system of Niederwaldstein lock up, under strict guard, in order to get the most out of cheap labour, long and time-consuming labour, but broken up, however, by peripatetic strolls, in a charming courtyard, where these workers relax, contributing with all their knowledge to the improvement of a certain elliptical, expressive and colourful slang that will no doubt serve as the bases of future languages, of Niederwaldsteinian roots, if the phenomenon, fortunately stopped for the moment, of barbaric invasions starts again. He showed them a very pretty staircase. The steps of harlequin breccia winding upwards with a band of mosaic climbed close to a banister in false mar-

---

1 Refers specifically to a Germanic court.

ble bristling with statuettes of polychrome sandstone, not white or blue, like basic sandstone, nor that awful dark Sienna or yellow ochre of old Flemish sandstones, but purple, orange yellow. Fat drinkers and large ladies as ample as goatskin bottles spread out, and from the ceiling there hung a chandelier with twisted multi-coloured ironwork like an improvised bouquet of wildflowers; small rooms contained a few paintings. The Major asked to see the Raphael; little Doctor Vana, annoyed, immediately opened a door, and as though in a chapel, in a well-lit room, tree branches adorning the window with a mobile and charming architecture in a luxury of red divans, framed with red and gold tapestry, a Virgin was holding a child. "Marvellous!" exclaimed the Major, then the King approved as did Sparkling, open-mouthed, whereas little Doctor Vana was thinking separately that in truth the famous Virgin really did have the appearance of someone going to market. "This canvas," he said, "is not from the Elector's personal collection; it was placed here at the time of the munificent annexation of 1815 at the behest of his very gracious majesty the ruling king, represented in this matter by Major-General von Backpfeife, superintendent of fine arts; my esteemed predecessor has often told me of Major-General von Backpfeife's taste for the paintings of Raphael, he was buying them from all the Jews in Berlin, and also from some in Glogau who, being aware of his specific taste for the seraphic painter, had made sure that they were in a position to supply them to him. I could not be certain that this one comes from one of these purchases; but I would be inclined to believe that, given its striking similarity to a Murillo,[1] that it is by Mengs,[2] the Saxon Raphael, who lived many long years in Spain, and was capable in his paintings of making combinations of the most delicate brush strokes, in the style of his two favourite masters; there are chances when a Raphael has this polychromy of porcelain that it is a Mengs, one of our glories; and is it not thoughtful to offer to your patron, instead of a Mengs worth a hundred écus, a Raphael worth thousands of ducats; Mengs was a good, patriotic Saxon." And indicating small panels in the corners of the illustrious chamber: "Here are other gifts of the king, from the same time, they are pastels by Liotard;[3] there are lots of them everywhere, especially in Amsterdam; people of high birth greatly esteem the works of this artist, I have never discovered the same sentiment amongst the painters, sculptors and pastel artists I have come into contact with through my duties; perhaps it is because their researches are not directed towards this type of painting, in which feeling is more important than technique." The Major seemed surprised by these allegations, King Christian remained indifferent and Sparkling only listened with one ear.

"Here is," said the doctor, "the real collection of Margrave Joachim Egbert; truth to tell, it was not really his own taste that brought it about; he quite willingly consulted a number of poets, and although

---

1 A seventeenth-century Spanish baroque painter.
2 An eighteenth-century German (Saxon) painter.
3 An eighteenth-century Swiss painter.

it is said that the poets of this country, during the last century, were only concerned about knowing where the greatest amount of cheap tobacco and the greatest amount of cheap brandy could be found, there were amongst them men of taste; the Margrave had excellent ones even though he paid them less well than his neighbours; perhaps because his neighbours set much store by their poets being able genuinely to establish a French-style tragedy and wanted from them the genre and general appearance of M. de Voltaire;[1] he on the other hand was keen that they could give some far off or rather expansive charm to a number of local products that the Margraviate excelled at producing; he contended only that they should enunciate clearly and in beautiful rhythms the virtues of French wines that the scientists knew how to manufacture in his distilleries, as well as his brandy which enjoyed a genuine reputation; it was genuine brandy made from quetsch plums. He also had the idea of celebrating in couplets a water that slightly cured all illnesses, and whose briny taste is still appreciated today; this water had, amongst other virtues, the advantage of attracting to this country foreigners who knew, beyond doubt, that the pharaoh was tolerated in our little country; by lending out military personnel that we got back mostly intact, but amongst whom the most damaged were able to acquire a certain glory, he obtained money and with

---

[1] Although nowadays primarily known for satirical short stories, particularly *Candide*, in the eighteenth century he was also known for writing classical tragedy in the style of Corneille and Racine, a genre regarded as a much more prestigious.

this money he bought pictures because he liked to surround himself with them; at some moments he would assert that painted people possessed better qualities for the future than living ones, because one day you may exchange them for lots of small royal effigies on highly desirable metals. And so he bought, advised by these (poets that he brought together in the evening in this tobacconist's shop that I will show you, where he spent moreover his best moments), the wonderful and so bright Mary Magdalene by Ribera[1] whose topaz hair trembles at the approach of the herald angel; here is a Rubens he was keen to possess," and the little doctor pointed to a Silenus[2] with pendulous breasts and a fat belly, bald, his skull furrowed like a fat stomach, that beautiful girls with strong, slender legs were lifting and carrying as they buffeted him in an ironic triumphal march. Little paintings by Roland Savery[3] in a slightly blackish flowering of tigers and fawns, playing alongside enormous white horses; doctors by Jean Steen,[4] sanctimonious and brilliant, were taking the pulse of large women adorned with lace and bedecked with jewellery. In a small canvas, drinkers in red smocks, with their pipes in their mouths, were gathered around pewter tankards on which danced a sunbeam and, on the ground, fat children were frolicking with large dogs. But the wonder of the room was a rare Vermeer of Delft; on a balcony, decked out with Turkish carpets

---

1 A seventeenth-century Spanish painter.
2 A companion of the god of wine Dionysus in Greek mythology.
3 Roelant Savery, a sixteenth- and seventeenth-century Flanders-born Dutch painter.
4 Jan Steen, a seventeenth-century Dutch golden age painter.

with purple and milky-white floral design tinged with blood and alabaster-like, a beautiful girl in a yellow dress, of a golden sunny yellow, was listening with a smile to the words of a few ladies' men and also to the admonition of a wrinkled shrew that was no doubt indulgent towards the handsome young men who were talking to her with hilarity; according to Doctor Vana it was the most important item of the museum and from time to time it was necessary to oppose its being taken for reasons of state from the little city of Pohlstock to embellish the beautiful rooms of the great museum of Gevehrstadt, capital of Niederwaldstein. The noble visitors accorded no more than a limited attention to the paintings, their eyes skimmed negligently past abundant panels in which minor Dutch masters reproduced their homeland, dark green, with murky water and skies that were definitively grey. They scarcely glanced at the exquisite bloodless face of the Meister des Marientodes[1] that the Doctor drew to their attention, and an energetic portrait of Scorel;[2] they wanted to make a start on visiting the museum of precious objects, particular relics of the excellent Margrave; they had heard about their choice, their weight and their price.

Sarmatian saddles with wide stirrups of perforated and ornamented metal, made of red leather braided with threads of gold, with turquoise and garnet lozenges, rubbed shoulders with daggers equally embellished

---

1 Possibly a reference to sixteenth-century paintings by Joos van Cleve.
2 Jan van Scorel, a sixteenth-century Dutch painter.

with precious and hard stones. Antique halberds and falchions, grouped in sets with guisarmes and cadors, highlighted with their metallic sheen and their brilliant trimmings, wide and roguish faces of ancestors, suspended on the walls above their points; with their wide, hard faces these predecessors looked like solid wood-cutters, having no ambition greater than to be very solid and very square; a little cunning in their eyes suggested at the same time that as well as being ruffianly soldiers they were astute merchants; the type was on balance robust and vulgar. One room was filled with old firearms; small models of culverins, cannons, antique rifle-cleaning brushes, pelicans with meticulous astragals, with pretty artillery drag-ropes, recalled in the middle of this museum of weapons of destruction, children's memories of recherché toy soldiers.

King Christian who prided himself on his knowledge of artillery, like almost all princes of Teutonic race, asked a question. "Ah!" said Doctor Vana, "at the time when all these toys were built Margrave Joachim Egbert was apparently occupied with miniatures. The date of this collection is scarcely later than that of the dolls and children's toys that it pleased him to put together in the next room," and the Doctor led his visitors into a rotunda with green walls adorned with mauve reflections, whose glass cases contained a spangled microcosm, a Lilliput of waxes and materials; polychrome players had their fingers stuck to amber chess pieces, fat bourgeois with powdered pony tails and pear-shaped bellies were hugging naked little girls. Large people, on whom rainbows had faded, were brandishing curious vermeil spoons in the direction of jade pots; half-opened houses were offering a profusion of small, fine accessories, and in them big, white, fat children were opening sideboard doors; one might have said a Pompeii of dwarves surprised by ankylosis and, in the centre, on a fine plinth, an illuminated piece of pottery, showed the venerable Margrave mounted on a barrel, with one hand holding a very fine pipe and with the other snapping his finger into space, at whom? Probably at his wife; it was into the adjoining tobacco salon that that Margrave was inviting his poets and his friends.

The tobacco salon was a fairly long gallery; the upright wall, of light oak, supported the twisting vaulting with beautiful mottoes in gothic characters, whose main message was to smoke in order to slake one's thirst and to slake one's thirst the better to be able to smoke, in the most ancient and most respectable gothic mode; coloured foliage snaked around couplets of wise men. It was a little, but with more solemnity and a perfect accent of virtue, the simple accents of our reed-flute players. A frieze of pottery bellies ran along the plinth. A reduction scale, situated in one corner, allowed one to measure out the corpulence, one face of which was, on this occasion, clearly captured; the Hamburg drinker surpassed by far every other sphericity, this famous drinker never having had in all his life any rival other than a famous Rotterdam brewer, struck down by apoplexy a short time before an inspired friend had had the project to gift this collection to the excellent Margrave; the latter had, moreover, relegated to the attics a few bellies of the North; in his opinion, the use of barley beer and white beer deformed this aspect of the human being, much more attractive when the well-worked hop of temperate zones succeeds in giving it the most aesthetic proportions. One should add that the Margrave had wished not to have in this collection a few rival and too neighbourly bellies, hostile abdomens that had gone against his very own through malpractices, through protective and aggressive customs duties. In that instance, as in all matters, the awful system which consists of going against nationalities the better to preserve dynasties had borne its guiltiest fruits.

For two thirds of the length of the opposite partition, as far as windows were concerned, the outer wall offered only and very high up small panes that were quartered as far as possible by tiny grey-coloured wooden slats; from the low, light-coloured wooden armchairs, set out in one single row, along a vast oak tables, one could catch sight of the horizon of clouds, grey clouds, like those which pass most often over Pohlstock, in the grey sky that is the attribute of Pohlstock, the other skies of varied hues, multi-coloured, sentimental, dreamlike, seemingly being in the pay of happier countries, or those possessing a more considerable budget. The low, light-wood armchairs were fixed to the floor; in their radius, a solid pewter decorated pitcher and a plate made of the same material were attached to the table by a short, solid chain. The pitcher was there to serve beer to the drinker, the plate was provisioned with tobacco, a narrow but very deep drawer contained long porcelain pipes, decorated with his illustrious portrait, that the Margrave gave to his liege-men, as later Napoleon lavished his portrait on tobacco-pouches, a portrait enhanced by diamonds; the Margrave was not giving out diamonds, but he was giving out tobacco. Truth on one side, truth on the other side, certainly dissimilar, however in no way mendacious.

But at the southern end of the tobacco salon a large bay-window opened its brightness on the gardens, swans gliding on lakes, and the collection of parrots, drawn up under the trees in military ranks; sumptuous curtains framed the beautiful window, and, without obstructing the light, a throne was taking radiance from it. The captives of the great table could see it just by turning their heads. The red velvet throne, supported by two gold-bearded Caryatids, the broad backrest convoluted with wood-nymphs with faces of macaque monkeys, served the Margrave as his abode when, every day, he presided over the revelry. In the evenings, with all affairs of state over a long time since, when the elected court had taken its place in the low armchairs, in front of the tankards, the Margrave would enter; a flowery pleated robe, with painted floral designs, glistening, short enough to reveal his cavalry boots passing by, this was his adornment. Mantillas of lace studded with jewels played around his neck; his head remained free and masculine. Then the Margrave would sit on his throne and from the rank of poets madrigals came forth; it was for him his supreme joy; he would laugh, sway, have the verses repeated, he would savour it, declaring that his Prussian cousin,[1] always occupied with his flute and his armies, had not the slightest idea of the frank and comic delights that a simple margrave, selling him soldiers as to anyone else furthermore, and at the same price, was inhaling, possessing as he did the spikenard and cinnamomum of the whole of his thinking country. And when joy, his own joy, was at its height, he would summon one of his henchmen, whose reputation was to transcribe French writers in a burlesque style as Scarron[2] did with Virgil; then blossoming, sending out the most marvellous rings of smoke from his fine porcelain pipe, his attention would melt and he would laugh with warm tears at a market Andromaque[3] or a farmyard Medea,[4] whatever his favourite cooked up for him.

Then he would essentially chuckle. "I, dear friends, only shackle your tobacco plate and your armchair. I seal off, it is true, your horizon, but on this point, I think that I am only conforming exactly to nature which, my masters, did not favour us; it has given us a tiny dormer window, open to a landscape that you embellish as best you can, you, the beauty in hops, you your dream of vines, you your dream of heroic medals, and other desires. If you belonged to my powerful neighbour, and redoubtable friend, you would have the lugubrious spectacle of seeing him enter your

---

[1] Probably a reference to Frederick the Great of Prussia.
[2] Paul Scarron, a seventeenth-century French writer who among other genres wrote burlesque epics.
[3] *Andromaque*, a tragedy by Racine, first performed in 1667.
[4] *Médée*, a tragedy by Corneille of 1635.

apartments and pester you with philosophy, just to see whether his orders, that decree that you would only be provided with the poorest candles, the saddest provisions, and decrepit furniture from the time of Luther, are being strictly observed.—Instead of a tiny dormer window in a joyful tobacco salon where your sovereign comes to take part in your discussions, you would be seeing tiny fortress dormer windows, decorated with good old galley slaves who would smoke without you; whereas here you are braving all these dangers, noticing a few of their charming mirages, which according to Lucretia is a joy, and you are free citizens receiving a pension as long as you sing after drinking. You turn your backs on the maxims of wisdom that I have expressly had painted on my wall, something which is also a reasonable allegory. The tankard and the muse are free in you, only the Pegasuses are slightly tied down, but who amongst you, oh poets, would mistake a chair for a Pegasus! As far as you others are concerned, my friends, you who are involved with affairs of State, study in me the vestimentary incarnation of our time, and do not complain; I know that you would not complain; a good citizen of Pohlstock is in need of a title and a decoration; you have them both; what more would you have with my powerful cousins and neighbours, except for the trouble of not knowing where to drink your beer, whereas here the State gives it to you, in the gracious company of the sovereign that you venerate."

And then the toasts multiply, the parodies start up again, sometimes interrupted by sentimental elegies, that made tears of laughter run down the face of the Margrave; sometimes in the garden, fifes would make loud, strident sounds, and the Margrave would pretend to be confused. Do you hear my cousin's flute, what are we going to do? No doubt run to arms! But we're so well off here; and the extent to which I have hired to him my good soldiers, so that I no longer know whether these worthy men would recognise me, what a war! What a war that would be! Ah! Frequently for the rest of us Coriolanus has returned home to Coriolanus.

Such was, according to Doctor Vana, the table banter characteristic of Joachim-Egbert. Sometimes an informal dance in the gardens forced his acolytes to put on a costume similar to his own, only a less splendid one, and the feast lasted into the night, with the pine trees and larches illuminated with the topaz-like splendour of the resin torches; it was ended by slow and long swigs of wine in the tobacco salon; and whoever might have tried to persuade Joachim Egbert that he was not creating there the sought-for Eldorado, the greatest possible feast of the greatest possible felicity, would have been received with a shrug and with contempt. Joachim was convinced. "Why," he would sometimes repeat into his pipe, "believe that your posthumous name, the real existence being prepared for the future, gains anything by the fact that, close to some village fountain, a nasty little bronze statue perpetuates your name trembling with a few kind epithets and lists of debatable victories. The name of the sovereign lasts better among his peoples if he provoked a long prayer to Dionysus amongst the wise and the elite. To walk good humouredly through the streets of the city whilst worrying about the price of provisions, to beat with one's own hand some rascal in the Alt-Markt and to hand him over to his great judge, to legislate for the happiness of a people who comply with the law at their convenience, or to be Solomon or to conquer like Louis XIV, what is the point of all that? One must amuse the people, amuse them again and again; where bread and money are concerned, they are perfectly capable of stealing these from one another, and the spenders recreate equilibrium once the fatality of old frugalities has been broken. Just go, sin and dance, laissez-faire, let people sin, let people dance, that is the motto of a good monarch." And, in fact, the good Margrave had well and truly lived by these turbulent mottoes.

"The only other thing I will now show you here," said the Doctor, "is the Napoleonic display. The great man was obliged, after Leipzig, to stop here for a night. Hitherto he had always been received here with the most absolute courtesy. There were outbursts of local patriotism. As soon as his drums were beating at the barriers, you could not have kept indoors one of our serious men, one of our small children, or one of our dogs. This local patriotism adorned our windows with the most charming ladies in scrupulously marvellous finery; but after Leipzig, we were overrun by general patriotism. The vanguards of Niederwaldstein, comprising patriotic Junkers,[1] possessed by the need

---

1 Member of the landed nobility in Prussia.

to rebuild themselves from the long privations of victory, were reimbursed from the cellars of the main palace and also from the reserves of this little palace. Generalised patriotism is much finer than localised patriotism, it cost us perhaps the lives of a few young men who enthusiastically followed the elites of Niederwaldstein, at their own expense mounted on their own horses and paid from their own pockets! But, as you are aware, patriotism does not count the cost. The very few that returned were honourably paid or pensioned off, except where liberalism was suspected; one was not playing with fire. And so these souvenirs of Napoleon that had been preserved here first of all to bear witness to his glorious visit, in relics, here a nightshirt, a sword-knot that he had replaced in our city, and his tiny slippers, bearing witness to future historians of the exiguity of his feet, these became the focus of curious, hostile and ostentatious pilgrimages for those from Pohlstock that had safely retuned from the light-infantry regiments of Niederwaldstein and also for the less favoured that had followed the army of our gracious sovereigns attached simply to equipment trains, or even to military canteens. These people, who had formed old comrades' associations, would come every year to gaze at what were the relics of the Emperor and had been transformed into the remains of the Usurper. The government sold them this favour for one thaler for four people; today I am only authorised to charge fifty pfennigs per person for each visitor, except when elections are on and entrance to these galleries is not only free but encouraged."

Major Langhirsch, rather shocked by the actions and language of the little doctor, was monopolising the King; but Sparkling was enjoying listening to these words spoken in a low and uniform tone.

It was evident that the Doctor had no thought of committing the crime of high treason. He was talking as he might have talked to his colleagues, that was all; and Sparkling was savouring this differentiation; Count Muller and Baron Schulze could hear everything. To a question from Sparkling, Doctor Vana replied: "Yes, Napoleon III did come. He wished to see the display with the relics of his ancestor. At the time I was a librarian in the main palace; it was by chance that I saw him here. His head was very inclined towards his shoulder and he had a fleshless pallor. He looked exactly like his medallions or his effigy on coins. He walked through the rooms, with a very shuffling gait, without posing any questions. His watery eyes did not focus on anything. He walked past the display he had come to see; we had to point it out to him. For a few minutes he lost himself in contemplation; no doubt he was thinking about something else, then he took fresh air in the garden and deigned to ask my revered predecessor a few points about the history of the kingdom of Westphalia; my predecessor who had been given this job for services rendered during the repression of miners' strikes, did not know much about these pages of our history, his rather jingoistic erudition resting rather before and after these sad events. And so he introduced me and I was fortunately able to reply to the few questions I was asked. The Emperor's tone was one of simple, infinite desolation. He had come without pleasure, he left without joy. The astonishment of the inhabitants of Pohlstock was such that, during his visit, no type of demonstration took place during his presence; but when the retinue had departed, taking him back to his temporary residence, they all spread out into the cafés, indulgently fabricating one to another the sort of conversations they wanted to have had with him and which form even today, through the self-interested toleration of them all, one of the bases of our legend."

The Major who had succeeded in leading the King away from this frivolous and rather insurrectional gossip, was marching along, rapid and unctuous, urgent and obsequious. Moreover, it was only too happily that Christian took off the mosque slippers that the rules had obliged him to wear. The Major was dragging him, with all his polished weight, towards other shores, but Sparkling thought he should invite the Doctor to join them that evening, which Christian agreed to despite the fact that it annoyed the envoy of his royal cousin.

That evening, a magnificent star-studded evening, an evening with only a few clouds so that the undulations of the sky seemed more magnificent, an evening of soon disturbed half-mourning, and already studded with numerous and pale and distinct gemstones, heading towards a small café towards the Zehl, Christian as if welded to the tall Major was discussing with him future phalanxes and incompressible and gigantic detonations, whereas Sparkling, remaining a little in the rear, was trying to dip into the mind of the little doctor.

"But tell me, kind Sir," said the good phalaena[1] of official joys, "what do you do on all the days of all the little life of the little town?"

"I tidy up, Monsieur le Baron, I tidy up; I have great difficulty tidying up my little museum; I write nearly every month a new report proposing its maintenance. I keep up to date, I read again my dear Brentano and the marvellous von Arnim, and the gentle Tieck;[2] I take part in tumultuous life by enjoying French novels, which allows me to foretell our own a few years in advance. I read and I tidy."

"But are you not afraid that this museum, which they contest your right to run, could be forbidden to you, and then, for I thought I have noticed with you, to my great pleasure, a freedom of language, rare, I believe . . . . . ."

"Oh! I only speak very rarely; most of the time I listen. I can hardly be suppressed; the day that the Fine Arts Council of Gevehrstadt no longer had to pass decrees about whether or not to conserve the margravial pavilion of Pohlstock, they would experience a profound void; I serve as a pretext as in my office, I do, humble as I am; and then they will not deprive my compatriots of their museum; they want blood tax and direct tax, that is enough; they are scarcely thinking about touching the tiny amenities of the little city. A few foreigners who bring with them a little money come here; if the museum were closed down, perhaps fewer would come and that would serve as a pretext to

---

1 Literally "a moth".
2 Brentano, von Arnim and Tieck were German poets.

the local commercial class to ask for a garrison, which is wanted neither by the aristocrats, who want to be peaceful, nor by the common people who are socialist.

"The antagonism of these three elements helps to keep me in place."

"Ah! Your common people are socialist, and what are they like, what do they say?"

"They don't say anything, they sing, in the evening in their own brasseries, or else they summon there a few instrumentalists armed with redoubtable brass instruments; as their cafés are exceedingly small, these brass instruments make a din. Sometimes a man of the people, a little saturated with beer, sprawls against the door which he pretends to mistake for his good wife and whom he is pitying with warm tears. The last to leave take him or carry him and reintegrate him with the lady he is whimpering about having left. From time to time, a local orator, a politician, comes to give them a very abstruse speech about social economics; by antiphrasis, no doubt, these speeches are given in the Tonhalle, our little concert hall; they are captivated and their attention is worthy of a better fate. If they don't understand it isn't their fault, the speeches are very moving. I never miss one of these lectures so much do I enjoy seeing them listen. They are like threadbare children who open their mouths for the holy bread. They do not receive very much!"

"But don't you think that the fact of taking part in these meetings could harm you?"

"Bah! Zurich is also a city, one is in good company; my small, personal library is lightweight; and who cares about Doctor Vana? And then we are heading towards socialism so slowly and surely that nobody is surprised to find a functionary far removed from the military profession attentive to its slow progress."

Christian and the Major were arriving at the Zehl talking tactics nineteen to the dozen; they had formed battalions completely in their imagination and had then prepared them for attack; once the position had been captured, they had solidly fortified them. A cavalry combat on the left had been a sort of digression; the morale of the troops had been excellent; where victory is concerned the morale of the troops is a major factor, and the generals asked for no more than to taste the lager beer of Pohlstock, whose reputation, without being universal, compared honourably with the Capuzinerbrau from Augsburg, possibly not quite as well, but Bavarian beer is more thirst-quenching than subtle local beers.

GEVEHRSTADT

I

THE express train was racing up gradients; Pohlstock station, with its garden of rhododendrons so artificial and bureaucratic, with its green-uniformed policeman, whose helmet looked at its base like a funnel-shaped cooking pot topped with a poker, despite the savage aspect of a scrap of imitation panther skin, was no longer but a dot in space; for a moment Pohlstock appeared again, surrounded by its shadowy parks. Pohlstock, its red roofs, its friendly belfries, the large entrances of its welcoming inns, looked amidst the darkish greenery like curious items of patisserie. The train reached the plateaus. It was like a libation of fresh air; on the flat expanse, nearer to a pewter sky, a few tins of Nuremberg beer could have been emptied; the most prominent and the closest together of these toys raised their caps at the thunderous passage. The express was rattling the little stations, like glass cages, in which there was the trembling chirping of a perpetual electric bell; employees were running, Tyrolean hats were no doubt exchanging routine thoughts about the equipment and the prestigious look of these luxury express trains, made for whom? For grandees, princes, important traders capable of buying the whole village just by putting their hand in their wallet, better, with a pencil mark on a scrap of paper; and the daily conversations, once the last coach had shaken the small hall, evoked golden cities with evenings of illuminated pleasures, twenty doors receiving in a sparkling of white light those who wished to see ballerinas; the stories evoked journeys through life, in flight, in youth, in passion, in far-off times; and the pipes were smoked more slowly, with regret, with vivid bliss or expecting a hazard, a chance, a windfall, to be able to go one day again along crowded pavements where the goods and beauties of the world are found in profusion.

Then it was admirable hills, the gentle curves of the beautiful breasts of Titanesses, where the express was running downhill, spitting and whistling like a band of howling urchins; lines of forests emphasised the horizon, grave crows were sampling the air two by two, colts were prancing in coquettish fear. The pretty villages, villages of pastel, wood and brick, oakwood, pink bricks, a salmon-coloured church with a copper cupola, one could have said that in other times they were decked with giants' quoits, cast negligently, through a midday of gemstones and young snorting of giants, on these gentle slopes, according to the hazard of an enormous game of discus throwing; and laughter had surged up to the sky so as to make it inalterably joyful, and the wand of Bacchus was living on in enormous, ripening bunches, by dry stone paths; the fertile prairie listened carefully for ever to bugles of triumph, to a vehement herd of bulls, and festive palfreys; the pewter sky seemed to have been left behind for ever.

And amongst the passengers on the express, swollen with business affairs or cares, factory or bank men, mechanically launched as if on curtain rods from one end of the railway lines to the other, nobody had ever dreamed of ending up in one of these villages full of clematis and wisteria, and winding muffled streets, to finish up there in a straw hat and slippers, watering can in hand, in the middle of a little garden, in front of the veranda of the Villa Wilhelmine or the Villa Monplaisir, and to doze off for a long siesta in a comfortable well-earned Thonet chair,[1] whilst the young girls in their high, coloured aprons are having fun on the uphill streets, with games, cries and laughter, and rackets. On Sundays they will go to the church, where the old statues of painted wood were the work of the hermit who defied Diana, and Satan, and the fairies; and in the evenings the organist comes to the house, to play a little profane music, and to get them to dance, to teach them how to sing old ballads with attenuated shivers and new lieder, and to celebrate beer, wine, the plighting of troths, the passing of handsome knights in the vines, and the spinning wheels of the poor girls, as well as the monotonous cantilena which filters between the waltzes, amongst the operettas. And the villagers, if they were aware of the fine, melancholic thoughts, and the song-thrushes of hope that sing

---

1 In the 1850s Michael Thonet had popularised bent-wood chairs, the most famous of which is the Viennese coffee-house chair.

like larks in powerful craniums, would alternate their statements about wanting to live in the towns where income runs in the streets, and they would begin again with their lament of damnation against the power that invented the division of labour, that wanted them only to be able to make the legs of a chair, whilst the back and the seat are manufactured elsewhere, far away, in a distant Mecca, to which they will never go, for the law that keeps them bent there, keeps them in place by the exiguity of their pay, and only allows them to be unemployed if they are sickly or untransportable.

The express entered a vast plain that sloped down gently towards the North. By a parsimonious nature of light the wide rivers revealed, on their banks, around heavy barges laden with bricks, close to materials piled up on the bank, a large muddy stain; a slow almost imperceptible lapping, coming from factory waste, was agitating the otherwise basically still waters; in the centre sometimes, between dense convoys of squadrons, an arrow of light left its trace, a memory of the water fairies who, for so long, dressed in green, sang whilst strumming the silver strings of their zithers. Long stations where workers were bustling to run behind wheelbarrows, buffets, postage parcels, then the plain began again, flat, with cereals and hovels, hillocks in the distance, villages with slate clock towers.

Major von Langhirsch was explaining to his two travelling companions, respectfully and clearly, how important this country was, this very country that for a long time had been the world's battlefield; it had been discovered as a result of carnage; carnage from the East and the West had intermingled there after the carnage and the pillage of the hordes that escaped through the woods, the hordes grazing on the country, through those coming from the East and the West; then the Sword had installed the Cross and had kept it in place; fighting and militant bishops had struck the old oak trees with the wood-axe and had killed the legends; their travels covered the lands and brought back from them fruits and animals for the monasteries; bells and wooden beacons warned them of the approach of the infidel. Marshes had served as discreet ossuaries for quite a few barbarians with shaved heads; with the guarantee of their huge amounts of arms negotiations had begun; the church and the warehouse had provided themselves with men at arms, and a tough race of victors had been established, greedy, harsh, courageous, impervious to fatigue, to spilled blood, serious and religious, with prayers after the butchery.

"These were," said the Major, "the beginnings of our royal race of Niederwaldstein. They started by being gallant knights; and on the savage march, as their first task, they cleared up the forest hiding places, the clearings with idols and savage brigands. The Margrave was relying on the men at arms as today the King does on his Junkers. They constituted, as you are aware, knights of the faith. Each one of these hillocks recalls one of their acts of heroism and piety. When the Reformation came, they were already, like tsars, popes and sovereigns over their domains; moreover, they were the treasurers of the whole surface of the country. The Reformation consecrated their rights; and if the men of this time had not been too numerous to be ambitious, tenacious and strong, the aim of those who embraced the new faith, in order to be men according to God, upright and solid in fixed principles, in the fear and knowledge of God, in full possession of their conscience, that aim would have been fulfilled; already for centuries the work would have been carried out, Niederwaldstein would have had its imperial sovereign in the image of God."

Sparkling was remembering the remarks of Doctor Vana, about the ineradicable instinct that would push the provinces, once the intoxication of victory was over, to turn in on themselves, to live their local life, to give up the responsibilities of grandeur; actually he did not share these opinions but could not contain himself from tackling the Major about particularistic tendencies.

The Major found this very funny; how could that be possible? You know only too well that these poor people because they were disunited, have been continually flogged by the winds of major wars. By bringing war to them, great enemy potentates were tacitly in agreement to spare their own domains and protect (he meant fleece) their subjects, uniquely themselves. These ancient wars were tourneys where they agreed to meet in the buffer-state, to live and to fight there. Now that the different strands of Niederwaldstein have been brought together, they are happy and peaceful. Wars will take place elsewhere; the more or less phony annexations have brought them a redoubling of prosperity; a strong people protects itself.

The King was thinking, separately, that the Major in his general goodwill for the small countries that must be defended and loved, was no longer thinking about the exact state of Hummertanz; annexation, protectorate, burdens, he found all that silly and onerous. For him nothing was less attractive than to be swallowed up; the politics he dreamed of consisted of being liked by all his neighbours, holding out, sparing them the trouble of fighting to establish the fate of his remains. To be the second in Rome, or to be even less than second, did not attract him. To be the head of a complete household is worth more than a major share in an association; and yet the facts were urgent; perhaps he would have to choose; not one of his powerful neighbours wished to swallow him up, but each one wanted to attach him tightly to themselves with benefits, treaties, and where possible a few good and strong garrisons. This slender Major seemed to be very hungry; he was no doubt a well-rounded specimen, chosen for this occasion from amongst his colleagues; the others must have been terribly similar, fanatical and insatiable. But Sparkling liked the Major enormously for he revived in his mind, through his words, his gestures and his silences, thousands of happy memories, of abundant caricatures. This officer seemed to him to be glazed, painted for parade, modified; with a light rubbing it ought to be possible to reveal the military and shopkeeper pilgrim; his joyful tastes both of a regularly turbulent life and of one tormented without mishap, were communicating to him some distance from the pietist reasoners of the sabre, of whom he detected the sharp desire to accumulate and the excessive proselytism; worth far more was this stateless Doctor Vana, asking for nothing more on the horizons than hops, tobacco and art collections.

At top speed, the express was now gnawing through the moors and heathlands; pine plantations in the distance were giving the appearance of forests; the hand of man could be seen in the regularity of the plantations. Pine trees for Christmas festivities rubbed shoulders with wood for burning, of which the last twigs turned their backs on wood for construction, whose sudden masses were making holes in the thick vertical curtain of the arborescence, then a corner of poorly cultivated plain, and children's playgrounds, lime trees, enormous horses, horses used for acrobatics that can support the large saddle on which pirouetting horsewomen balance, and then the wood, the plantation began again. As they rushed without stopping through stations, villages were scarcely noticeable, sometimes a distillery was steaming; the few human beings visible under the sky that had become pewter again, were dressed heavily, coarsely, as if in leather. One knew that there were in the surrounding countryside heavy, melancholic castles, with a sad and surly rococo style with enormous halls, with evocative and mysterious woodwork, with large iron balconies and vast, mute windows looking over lead-coloured lakes; flights of herons were the only things trembling in the air; and legends had princesses dying of languor, or sometimes taking, on purpose and through despair, seeds of mortal illness, close to ponds that were taciturn and seemingly remorseful, against whose opacity reflection died. The empty castles had formerly been illuminated, on hunting days, by the fire from enormous chimneys where the venison was piled up; gradually they had been abandoned, and old princes, old ancestors lay there, the most often these times, allowed themselves to be forgotten there with an oblivion that was not broken by any invitation to appear in Gevehrstadt; sometimes princes of royal line had come there to die, always prematurely; and suddenly there returned to the King's memory the far-off provincial manor-house isolated in the sands that were almost the same as these, in the animal and vegetable solitude of the poorest cantons in existence, the manor-house to which the Queen had retired to mourn her son; a sad, disquieting manor-house, a worry for the King who never wished to return there since he had taken there a sick sister; what was the Queen doing tiring out horses or singing out to a virginal. Sparkling also was struck by this similarity of landscape thought, but in a very different way, about the same people; to what could the Duchess of Sparkling be possibly bringing civilisation in these surroundings, and how the austerity of her stay must be elevating her taste.

The plain thinned out, a vague, grey line of houses was visible; perhaps one or two domes jutted out; then a large, treeless plain like an exercise ground; a café with children's swings on which soldiers were swaying, meagre inns, a small, dirty street with, in the brutal indiscretion of the train passing behind the houses, an exhibition of sordid, tattered clothes along washing lines, women in camisoles, brats bawling out, then majestically the train slowed down, skidded to a stop, it was Gevehrstadt. The city with twenty churches, thirty barracks, the capital of Niederwaldstein; the enormous, improbable city created through stock-market speculation and victory, astonishing in Europe, like a city transplanted from overseas, like an American city that had turned its back on the most recent progress and could have been banished here, in these primordial sands, alongside cold rivers.

The landau that was collecting the travellers, accompanied by a young prince charged by etiquette to welcome them at the station, jolted for a moment then fell in behind a magnificent squadron of bodyguards, white and silver, who were making their way, placidly, towards some guard of honour. Scarcely past this impediment, it had to speed off between small groups of uhlans in dark greatcoats. Without stopping it went past the facade of the new Parliament Building that was well situated between a small infantry barracks, a cavalry headquarters and a small telegraph office, all of which were ready for the prompt carrying out of one of those coups d'état, the basis of representative politics of the country of Niederwaldstein. Along the pavements it came close to the graceful Arsenal building, whilst on the other end of the Allée des Platanes, a crowd, arms swinging, agitated, was marching triumphantly in front of the military band of an infantry division; finally it was the Palace, its outbuildings studded at equal distances by grenadiers. Opposite, the buildings of the royal museums, copies of Italian palazzi or Greek aedicules,[1] shivering under the pewter sky. Siegfried Gottlob, the still youthful emperor, was waiting for his guests in the marble hall, a cross between an atrium and a tepidarium.[2] Twelve white statues of old margraves gave a comprehensive summary of all the information the modern world possesses about the musculature and the armour of the ancient Spartans and of the Romans that were the oppressors of the world. Only the faces authentically conformed to the glorious memories of the race of the Eisenfahrts[3] even though they may have been agreeably enhanced by laurels. Bald heads like those of the Caesars alternated with wigs like those of Louis XIV; it was decidedly only the facial angle that remained a true likeness according to the genealogical modus. It was of widespread dimensions and notably snub-nosed. Between these statues, shields and banners taken from the enemy both hereditary and occasional; Niederwaldstein had waged war so often, either for its moral greatness (with the aim of annexation), or for its greatness of dignity (with the aim of subsidies).

On the ceiling well-dressed angels and draped winged women were sounding their great trumpets around tables of the new law, "wherever I have placed my foot, there is my new land". On the archway, snatches of military songs, the verses as it were of old regimental marches, embodied here the emotion, for these feudal gladiators, of the past, from stage to stage;

---

1 Miniature temples.
2 A warm room in an ancient Roman bath.
3 It is not clear who Kahn is referring to here.

and for this purpose Siegfried Gottlob had embellished the insignia, restored by the most conscientious of the archaeologists, of the recently reconstituted order of the Knights of the Lion, an order that had formerly expired in misadventures. The helmet and the silver breastplate created the heraldic image with the long ermine cloak; the sword looked as far as possible like Charlemagne's. Quickly King Christian was elected to a high rank amongst the knights of the order and Sparkling to a more modest level.

Grave and measured words, of an abstruse plurality of interest, adorned the first minutes of the official reception, and the two sovereigns retired together, to become simple mortals.

To benefit from the freedom allowed to his lower rank, Sparkling walked off through the wide, cold streets. Ah, what an improvement since his previous visit; the rue des Gendarmes still led to the rue des Canonniers close to the Place des Cuirassiers towards the Jardin des Pontonniers,[1] but where he remembered hovels there were now tall halls of brasseries like synagogues even more Moorish than Alhambras, with huge Venetian chandeliers, dedicated to Electricity. Near the Eglise de la Garnison[2] the crowd of children was swaying as it always does around market stalls of charcuterie and cooked sausages; the crowd of unarmed soldiers was strolling slowly from one end to the other of the ironic Allée des Détaillants,[3]

---

1 Soldiers responsible for building bridges and pontoons.
2 Garrison.
3 Retailers.

with its so slender trees; the river, so tiny beneath the enormous bridges, was not any more beautiful, only the statues on the bridges had gained a fine glaze. The Rathskeller was where it had always been; still where it had been is perhaps an exaggeration, for its place of origin was central; it was around its vast halls of honest and copious deliberations, around its sanctuary cellars, honest and copious libations, during which the fine and ruddy male bourgeoisie debated the fate of the world; now the Rathskeller is still in the same place, but the city has moved; the sanctuary of white beer is no longer the location of choice; there are similar ones in the flat, dirty and far-off suburbs. Nevertheless, the foreigner who sits down in these places honoured by the old name of an alderman engraved in gold letters, will always hear, if he listens carefully, the same conversation as before, weighing up the chances of war and the price of provisions. The deep cellar worthily fulfils its responsibility of municipal phantom, of old German burghers. And the wives of those who sit in the deep cellar? It is in the zoo close to the town in the summer brightness that chairs are bristling with crochet hooks and knitting needles. Often a dairy claims their attention, and it is around its tables, green with hope, that to the children gathered there they continue the lesson they have started in front of island birds, the large tawny ones, the captive eagles and the numerous pachyderms. To teach through entertaining! And besides since one comes at fixed times to see the lions and tigers being fed (the crowd becomes more colourful with a few soldiers since elsewhere the monkeys are going to be teased), shameless as everywhere, without respect for the glorious capital; but more than elsewhere one gets the small children to admire the moving sea-lion who displays his joy as soon as his regular keeper arrives. There is in his attachment a whiff of the old virtues of the race of Niederwaldstein that are being highlighted.

And the roads leading to this graceful zoo, green and cold like an English park, are being wandered along by groups of ladies walking slowly; they are going, they are coming back, and helmets alternate with shakos, patrols on horseback, with those on foot, there is a sudden stir, the crowd runs, it is Siegfried Gottlob in one of his military uniforms, who is making a showy ride around the woods flanked by aides-de-camp. Fifes and drums, drums and fifes, military bands, columns of troops, columns of passers-by chatting along the wide walkways, from the large Brasserie to the large Garden!

The evenings of Gevehrstadt bubble with felicities, but they are all the same. There one can hear music whilst drinking beer or whilst drinking wine, vocal or instrumental emanations; one may hear lighter music, made more complex by a few appearances of acrobats and trapeze artists; one may, still drinking, see English ballets or Italian ballets. One may also hear music and see French ballets, but only in the theatre; it is also a chance to familiarise oneself with the appearance of soldiers of the Guard, at rest, no longer martial but conquering.—What Sparkling was fearing was meeting in his box Siegfried Gottlob's Palace Marshal and noticing again how his purplish bald head showed beads of perspiration upon the arrival of the first ballet dancer, seeing again the profile of the artillery general, whose eyes automatically moistened at all the andante phrases, and the chamberlain spying on the figures and the bows and the same speeches (to swell the dossier he is compiling, at spaced out periods, of the anonymous mystifications that awake the capital like a terrible noise of cats meowing), or even the beautiful woman, professional beauty,[1] who looks as if she has been carved by Canova out of a slab of Emmenthal cheese, and she who has been gathering for so many years the last words[2] of so many Kapellmeisters, and retained from them a heroic and knowing air, of a youth that remained Sevillian, and so many others who lord it over arms, arts, fur trades, monopolies, unique warehouses and the formidable iron-clad chests of the iron-doored cellars, where are keeping watch, captive and terrible, proletarians with a colt revolver in their fists; no! This was too non-specific a décor, too universal capital-like, too cosmopolis with reserved squares, and to this solemn boredom Sparkling preferred the small titillation of pleasure that seems to glow in simple locales devoid of pomp.

As he was walking along the Allée des Platanes, on this warm and starless evening, Sparkling spotted the Mirabilium.

The Mirabilium was a collection of primitive and special astonishments. Once you were past the inevita-

---

1 In English in the text.
2 In Latin in the text "ultima verba".

ble ticket office, you reached it by a staircase fashioned in a grotto; in it, variegated lights illuminated touching scenes of love and abandonment that took place in mythical times, when things took place in grottos. A dark waxwork miscreant, brown and flinty, represented Kaïn[1] climbing far-off slopes and confronting the knight Tannhäuser who was tired of Venus. Once you had come out of that enchantment you entered a comic corridor crowded with all varieties of distorting mirrors, those that broaden the face, those that can make it narrower, those that hollow it out, those that inflate it, and rare varieties that crush the middle of the body whilst increasing the extremities; it was a joy for the good burghers of the town to stay here to watch the flight, as they passed rapidly by, of the ladies moved to indignation by this manifold outrage.

Next, lamentable, in a recess, there was an exhibition, in waxwork shapes, of a café room which represented Olympus for the beautiful minds of Gevehrstadt. A subtle allegory of things! These beautiful minds that were, when the room was inaugurated, brand-new and glossy, just as in life their glory interminably gave birth to their glory, were now faded, as were today their models, overwhelmed with the heavy twilight of decline. On the foreheads of these lined faces the irony of fate had left in place the hair they had before, their fleece of fuzzy hope, the abundant yellow hair of dreamed-of gold, and Sparkling, sometimes melancholic, that the spirit of decrepitude shaped more than any other at a

---

1 A character of reputed ugliness.

lamentable moment, thought he saw, seated at table, the areopagus, the future undertakers of those glories that Fate might just have rigged on their heads, above the everyday and impersonal black garb.

He had a happy diversion by the miniature sight of the flood.

In a limestone tub, spiky with lace-like rocks, spear-shaped ruggedness, scraps of plaster material embedding pieces of ore in a frame of grey fungi, a pathetic group of old men and children stretched out their arms, there climbed snakes, ichtyosauruses and a whole fauna of children's toys.

An attendant was supposed, once enough people had paid him a surcharge, to get the waters flowing and to empty into a reservoir the cataracts of an outlet. At this moment, not enough enthusiasts having come together, the desolate companions of gypsum looked rather as though they were burning up with polydipsia[1] and this upset the spectator attracted on the other hand by the chamber of horrors.

The chamber of horrors, despite the redundancy of its name, and its aim of striking the most sensitive organs of the commercial traveller and the jobbing workman on feast days, was nothing more than a brown room, surrounded by glass cabinets in which death masks and hands of plaster alternated their pale preparations; they were, according to the informative poster, criminal faces and hands of those who had broken backs, had brained people, stranglers, skirt chasers, those with axes, daggers and drugs.

---

1 Excessive thirst.

A knowledgeable Italian criminologist had provided the document, had sprinkled the moralising room with details, patched up ignorance and lacunae; nevertheless a certain scepticism had been seen amongst the ruling classes, less gullible about the story on show than the serfs, and it was a current joke to broadcast this myth: when the administration was not able to procure the masks of major criminals (the common ones were as easy to find as Shrovetide revellers) made up for the deficiency by using the effigy of aged tenors and of tragic actors who had ceased to move people, those who had never been able to grace major stages, and had only ever strutted their stuff in small towns.

Elsewhere there were, under domes, in glass cages, the young fiancée dressed all in white who is dying, orange blossom in her hands; the dying soldier, convulsed, still holding his rifle, his hand on his heart, his eyes blinking and his chest made to rise and fall by clockwork; the waxwork lady, so elegant, who is turning her back on you as she emerges from a narrow corridor and sends a greeting to a lady companion, ethereal and leaning smiling from a loggia, both of them captivating with their soft slenderness; the inevitable employee to whom requests for information are inevitably addressed, a joyful puppet show of ill-assorted sovereigns, a Frisian woman, Algerian women, children trapped in snow, and in one corner, under an almost unattractively falling material, could Sparkling believe his eyes! The old ancestor, the unpardonable blind man relegated there, all alone, with no retinue;

oh yes! With a retinue; his old chancellor, still living but dilapidated, coarse outlaw with a moth-eaten hussars' jacket, was disappearing a little further away in the darker half-light.

Ah! No doubt, in the State buildings and the military museums, where any displacement of great heroic canvases and of costly daubs involves so much expenditure, the old supports of Niederwaldstein had to retain their venerated place. When once one has had a whole gallery daubed with glory, battles and apotheoses, one thinks about starting again; and yet a shadow passed across Sparkling's face; these great pictures were not frescoes; destructible, no one thought of that, obviously, but moveable, it was possible that they thought of that; and with the memory of Christian coming back to mind, he smiled at the thought of a Christian relegated to the attic whilst a joyful inheritor devoured his income, the residues of his major business affairs and of his colonies, of a Christian pale, faded, relegated to the outbuildings, the common rooms, the school council rooms. Sad! Sad! Where do they go, these dominant heads and bemedaled chests of their owners! Finally! Large rooms, other ones, could still wrap in the folds of flags the colossal statues of the predecessors. And Sparkling walked, got slower and slower, explored the expanses bristling with unimportant figures, the decorated walls, the corners the adjacencies, without seeing anything else anywhere other than, glazed, pretentious, brand new, alone or surrounded by his staff, alone or surrounded by his family, alone or with the Queen, alone or with his allies, dressed as a hussar, as a Knight of the Order of the Lion, helmeted, breast-plated, simple, lavish, dressed down, good-natured, as a Tyrolean hunter, as a man of war, of home[1] or of romance, but always *eminent*, even more *alone* by being surrounded, liturgical, unique and papal, Siegfried Gottlob, the son of his fathers.

Ah! So passes the glory of the world, and this fashion that decreed that during their lifetime the old King and his Minister should preside over every festival with their statuary image, with their moulding, with their features painted over those of their predecessors; that they should be the companions of all festivals and the reminder of duty during the greatest pleasures; the courtly mode was disappearing and covered their memory with its image-reversing irony.

And yet they had come there, during their lifetime. Sparkling remembered that, when he was still a young man attached to some mission, he had wandered there, respectfully behind their heels and admiring their tallness and broad shoulders; the old King had wandered, glanced at the deluge, the corner of Grenada, the horrors and the emotions; he had sat at the buffet to praise the white beer, he had tried to compare his stature to that of a giant fed and displayed by the house, a giant Slav, scarcely taller than him if this Tartarus of exploitation were stripped of all artifice; it was even said that the impresario who was expecting some large royal generosity, having expressly closed his doors to

---

1 The word "home" is in English in the text.

the public, had only been reimbursed by nothing more than the total of the entrance tickets, exactly what he would have taken if instead of forty overbearing characters he had received forty wretches, but how important is gossip!

Oh ephemeral glory, informal irony, snowy thoughtlessness of things! And saddened Sparkling came back from there to the galas.

PARADES AND CATASTROPHES

I

ALL the pallor of the night had squatted over the frightful heathland, and the voice of the storm could be heard in squalls, and white flashes of lightning were ripping apart the phantom-like wall of mist, caused on the horizon by the sick waters of the emptiest and most desolate of plains possible, prisoners amongst the sickly, humiliated heather. The impatient rage of the wind was creating some groaning noise in the meagre shrubs, poor plantations which a clever forestry cultivation was trying to shelter from the meagre hares who race away from their castles of dry sand at the slightest footstep that invades this solitude, when there descended the main staircase of the Château de Thieve, the *Feldzeugmeister* and the *Kriegsingenieurs*, who were to construct, not far from there, on the Lugenfeld Plain, an entrenched military camp. A letter from King Christian had given them their accreditation to the Château de Thieve, close to the Queen, and their heavy carriage was taking them back, after a journey of ten kilometres, the frontier having been passed a few hectometres back, to the terrain they were studying. They wanted (on a whim) to stop for a moment at the only inn in the village of Thieve that, not far from the castle, was constructed of many rammed-earth bricks, and to spend time good-naturedly amongst the lugubrious revelry of this Sunday evening. The only inn contained melancholic intoxicated drinkers, and the beribboned bows of archery competition winners were standing unsteadily in the corners of the room. Tall and slim, the leader of the mission, wearing an almost black figure-hugging military greatcoat on which gleamed lacklustre medals, smiled when the youngest of the officers, conforming to the custom of the area, held his glass of beer out to the servant girl so that she could be the first to moisten her lips, then, when the young officer, in the same style, managed to have a conversation with a few of these ponderous retarded guests; thus they had the proof that immigration was beginning, that the vagabonds of his people were leaving, as pathfinders, towards this evil land, in the hope of what profits? And about their role, he did not really want to be sure since this was not part of his responsibilities. When the storm had calmed the major part of its anger, they stood up, and their heavy carriage set off at walking pace through the streets of the town, so as not to crush the natives who, haggard, were swaying before the walls of small white stones, then at the corner, on the road lined with birch trees, it bore them off at a galop; and the postillions, from time to time, were shouting out so that their rapid pace should not encounter, to their detriment, some heavy cart, without bright lanterns, full of sleeping louts, that their horse is bringing back at his slow pace towards the neighbouring hamlets; and during their journey, with sparse words, touching on the warm welcome at the Château de Thieve, the distinguished appearance of the Queen of Hummertanz, the beauty of the Duchess of Sparkling, the bizarre fantasy of living in this manor-house way out in uncultivated land, close to an abandoned military training camp, the thoughts of these guests of Thieve were preoccupied with their business; they had seen the success of all their attempts, and the success of their spying structure represented in this country (so poor that its inhabitants travel leagues to go further South, during artillery practice, to look for lead that has gone astray, even when the firing is still going on, in order to resell it), by bands of semi-brigands, semi-beggars and terrorisers of far-flung villages and isolated houses, whilst in Krebsbourg they skilfully managed the appearances of a myriad of droll characters in their pay, half-Hungarian, half-Triestine, sly people of races found by chance in capital cities, looking like managers of money, presented as Jews, often actually being Jews, when it was useful to embellish their filth with their attendance at the synagogue, but having the same relationship to Hillel or Heine as the wenches that intoxicated the sailors in the suburbs of Palos, before the departure of the great caravels, had to Christopher Columbus. Thieves were not kept in Niederwaldstein, they were sent abroad, on this peaceful crusade of civilisation; from this flowed two clear benefits, to impoverish the neighbour, to have documents, and also through their contact to contaminate the genuine, true revolutionaries that were exiled for good, and who were suffering from the proximity of these rogues, when they were not suffering the consequences of their not very far-sighted denunciations.

And whilst their carriage was travelling away, and the last light was going out in the village of Thieve, in the castle the Queen was weeping, with the newspaper wrappings quickly torn off as soon as the guests had departed, for the news had the serious face of forecasts of misfortune.

The terrible news was not that Papegay-Garten might once more have harangued the crowds, and shown them the frontiers torn apart, the powerless fortifications, and a group of hefty, beringed Croesuses grinning over the snake-like rest of those supposed to be the elite, nor the neighbour from the South, soberly announcing that a few garrisons on the frontier would be reinforced, nor the bands of pariahs, raising from the ground the circular fittings of plane-tree stipes, to use them to strike an armed force too weak authoritatively to close their meeting house, nor the prediction of a mad nun throwing herself, half naked, under the dark sky, across the chatter of the carillons, howling like an inconsolable Hecuba gasping as so many poor sacrificed goats were calling for terrible vengeance and as the scythe of fate was wiping its thread on the priests of Hummertanz, nor the acquittal of the pamphleteer whose last pages had made detailed revelations about the flaws of the dynasty, but this new one: that the incognito journey, the holiday, the restful trip, was turning into an official visit, with parades and reviews, and that King Christian had climbed the stairs of the Château de Saint-Hubert which was also, like this one, built in isolated heathland, in the middle of dark pine forests, a castle of gloomy memory where the most pietist ambushes had taken place, where the most sanctimonious ruses of the Eisenfahrts had triumphed. Slightly related, she knew their breed, and her whole loyalty was rebelling from any duty of her crown, against these pastors with prayers of iron and bullets, and who congratulated themselves piously on the destruction of Babylon, and the terrible blow struck against Moloch, whilst speculating about increases in the war chest.

And as the blond Duchess, surprised by this nervousness, was trying to modify the gloomy course of ideas to which the Queen was abandoning herself beneath the lamp, in this rotunda with its balcony, facing North with its view limited by such a platitude and destitution of the land, and unwisely was saying "that the news of the kingdom was good"—of the kingdom, perhaps not, but possibly of the King, but instead of the kingdom say henceforth the House of Commerce.

And to the surprised Duchess, this flighty woman for whom every mechanism was something sacred, owing to the fatigue she might have experienced examining it . . . There were suddenly across the pale building with its white panels, noises of bumping and jerky footsteps; shrill, strident cries were heard, in the heavy air of the long corridors, arriving very quickly from far away; and pale, court etiquette put slightly on one side, a major-domo entered. The Queen understood and quickly followed the torchbearer into the vast hall where her sister-in-law Queen Margarete, pulling out whole handfuls of her short, grey hair, was upbraiding portraits with tears and howls, a mad look on her face, full of fury, with bloodshot eyes, the madness of her fists agitating the torch; and the husky howls flew off into the silence, like cries of ghouls, and her footsteps resounded in an ardent trampling, in the normal silence under this vault; and in the incoherent harangue to the dead, whose flat effigies, still adorned with the official smile that masked the duplicity of their lips, were hanging on the walls, cast offs of old armies, or duplicates of false torsos of leaders of soldiers, princelings with the attributes of a bazaar, her voice was thundering out in diatribes and commands. Vague songs alternated with the sad modulation of the word Fire! Fire! Fire! Articulated as a military command, or in a heart-breaking manner, with great furious outbursts forwards or the gestures of a child cowering before the grip of a danger.

And when the Queen came in, white, her onyx eyes blacker beneath her smooth grey hair in headbands, taller in stature and calm in appearance, the mad woman crouched down, threw the torch down on some tapestry, and obliquely opened the window to throw herself out. It was the Queen herself who caught hold of her, on her own, the lackeys having suddenly taken on the appearance of a group of performers with walk-on parts in the theatre looking with a heartbroken gaze on the catastrophe, in which they must not get involved. The mad woman was struggling and it needed all the strength the Queen had acquired from horse riding to restore her, swearing and stunned, into the hands of the valets who had suddenly become emboldened, and the Queen's blood was trickling down her face.

She did not recommend silence. This Amazon living without her partner maintained her pride and drops of heroic blood, despite the apparent origins of her parents, landgrave-burgomasters in tolerated neighbourhoods. Legends recounted a triumphal passage of Napoleon across the little principality. Besides, she was keenly aware of her political inconsistency amidst this population of traders; as far as doubting that the most apparently faithful of these hairless faces of valets would go, as soon as tomorrow, to negotiate the exclusive story of a new outburst of madness of Princess Margarete, she knew the country only too well and especially the pasty-faced and wily clientele the all-powerful clergy surrounded itself with to doubt it for a moment. It was with a firm footstep that, with the blood wiped from her face, she climbed the steps of the painted wooden staircase with its colours of flowery marble, to be present when the poor mad woman was put to bed in her padded chamber and who was growling, like a sick child, tired, exhausted, at least for a moment no longer having before her eyes the terrible sight that had provoked her collapse.

The husband of the mad Princess, a blond colossus from the North, ambitious and unused, she also ambitious, and believing that his shoulders were broad enough to bear all burdens, they had accepted from the hand of the high powers from whom European equilibrium hides all dynastic conventions to reign over this terrible and turbulent region of Sagontide, where no sovereign had been able to last, where after six months kings were sent back to their palace by the guard company, where republican ministers received on the steps of the parliament building stones in their faces or revolver shots in the nape of their necks. The last episode of the regular expulsion of kings had had the strange feature that the guard company remained faithful; it was through the palace outbuildings that the rebels got in, vague troops commanded by or rather furnished with an old Marshal whose curriculum vitae showed his presence in all war offices, in a slow upward progress towards those of the minister. It was in this office, when a revolution was taking place, that he had himself signed his nomination as a Marshal, and made powerful by this title, that had been recognised by the republicans, he had subsequently organised the restoration of a monarchy with the name of some Bourbon who was deep in debt. It was after the republican regime that had overthrown this Bourbon that King Gerhardt had come to the throne, and he had lasted some time thanks to the happy idea he had had to create immediately a foreign legion, which was really a small army chosen from his compatriots, and continually swollen by people who came from the North, as workers, and after a week, not having found work, had joined his guard. The Niederwaldstein Minister took responsibility for sending him recruits and non-commissioned officers. And so, the first riots were repressed with methodical care. The populace could not get over its stupefaction. Hitherto the breaking of a few windows was enough to bear witness to the will of the people and authority would change hands; now genuine rifle shots scattered the crowds gathering at crossroads to demonstrate, and the capital had to conceal its anger beneath the threat from the canons in the citadel. But the muzzled and fearful animal did not delay in finding new resources for bringing power under control. They might have agreed to the authority of King Gerhardt, which was wise on the whole and mild enough to grant amnesty to the rebel prisoners a few days after the uprising; these indolents, used to smoking nonchalantly by the sea, or in the shade of trees, used to exchanging their opinions the length and breadth of the markets or in the deep porches of the churches, might have stayed quiet if the invasion of tax farmers, bankers, brokers, the whole lugubrious high command of industrial monopolisation had not pounced on this unfortunate country to suck up all its vital energy. Yet, it so happened that the praetorian guard, quickly won over to the gentle manners of the country, to its laziness, its games, its wines, only retained an artificial faithfulness to the powers that be. They might have defended Gerhardt, but not his new acolytes.

Then, one torch-lit evening of clamour, when the elite of the faithful troops were fighting in one part of the province against an uprising of clerical origin, Margarete, powerless, on her balcony, saw, seized by an armed crowd, King Gerhardt who had gone out with a few men to try to prevent the hanging of tax and exaction advisers in front of the palace. The populace having grabbed him, his arms of a colossus held tight by ten hands, wanted him to witness the quick death of his councillors for whom any noose was judged to be good. Where he was concerned, they accorded him the terrible honours of a military death, and he fell pierced by the bullets of a firing squad, in front of the great balcony of the palace that had already been invaded, where rioters were keeping Princess Margarete so that she could witness the whole spectacle. And it was the sinister order of the riot, the impersonal voice that had given orders to the tools of murder that, for twenty years her voice, childish or furious, had been roaring out or modulating.

And beneath the benevolent gaze of the Queen, leaning on the shoulder of the Duchess whose blonde appearance still seemed misty with disobedient fright, Princess Margarete slept in her padded chamber, with its carefully boarded-up windows, in the ironic pomposity of a bed so sumptuous that it looked like a catafalque, amidst the dolls she had smashed all day long, for, before her fit of madness, she had adopted and covered with her exclusive good graces a log of wood that she had dressed in a bonnet with green ribbons.

II

AT HUBERT-SCHLOSS, a poky little castle with impassable waxed stairs without the slightest scrap of carpet, enormous parsimoniously furnished halls with no other trace of hangings than a few distemper paintings on its good walls, solid enough for a good dungeon; views of a beautiful, flat parkland, where rotundas of water were surrounded by well-pruned yew trees, with reflections of statues eaten away by moss, so that Harpocrates[1] seemed to have permanently fixed to his lips the wherewithal to make a herbal tea, and that the wings of Mercury looked like an anthill of aspergillus and the lice that go with it; at Hubert-Schloss that had been a hunting pavilion in the style of Louis XIII before being built higher in the style of Louis XIV and receiving the definitive finishing touch according to the taste of Louis XV, following designs helpfully provided by good old Hodiz,[2] but first of all poorly reproduced by his copyist and by the

---
1 The god of silence.
2 Possibly a reference to Albert Joseph von Hoditz (1673-1741), a German aesthete.

Sarmatian who had been obliged to hew the stones following these summary indications, it was here that King Christian was wasting away; for it was nothing but hunts, brusque departures, in the uniform birchwood, rustic collations, and, from time to time, once every twenty-four hours, a railway trip to neighbouring towns, to scare the garrisons.

The very reasonable General de Loiseau de Echtenstein, writer, author of the tragedy *Saul* and, moreover, of *My Hours in Reflection*, four volumes, in octavo, slaved over during his rest periods, moreover Minister for War, was multiplying the movements of troops around Hubert-Schloss, to facilitate the royal forays, and Christian came there as well, although in no way did he experience the same joy as Siegfried Gottlob in shivering in informal dress, on a parade ground, in small towns, close to the more or less decorative standpipe statue of Ascanius[1] with his iron teeth, or of a Bertrand the founder, all of them hydraulically powered. But Siegfried Gottlob liked doing it and it was with such a tone of authority, the roughly awakened troops sent back to their original sleep, that he would murmur; here are the passive bayonets, that sleepy Christian was returning almost contentedly to Hubert-Schloss; for there were close to dynasties good passive bayonets, and his new uniform of Honorary Colonel of the Foot Grenadiers (regiment number six) was not unemployed.

Sparkling had his share of the honours, of the white beer, of the terrible stairs and of tea, standing in the

---

1 The legendary King of Alba Longa and son of Aeneas.

great drawing room full of grumpy ancestors (Pilotys[1] according to the prints, unmarked Winterhalters,[2] a Heim[3] on the move, a fixed Schlüter[4] bronze) and, above all pleasures, a decoration. However, to the gracious frolics of Monsieur the plenipotentiary Minister of the court of Hummertanz to that of Niederwaldstein, implying what pleasure the representative and the *persona grata* experienced in witnessing the touching agreement and what union was enriching with bliss the two sovereigns, he felt it necessary to reply: "Indeed, he has not yet been asked for his trousers and yet he has very fine ones; I think that if he is nominated, for anything may happen, Honorary Colonel of the Court Light Horse, he will have, like them, fine orangey gaiters that will console him for what he is losing in exchange." The Minister went away scandalised, with an offended air, which allowed another Minister of similar style to take him seriously for a minute, and these gentlemen who until then had found one another silly, sorted Europe out in their fashion that very evening.

And it was on the evening of this day that the Duke of Sparkling tried to explain to his sovereign what sharp practice of his people he was tempting with these greedy men; he proved to him that to deliver the country to them in order to save the crown was unholy

---

1 Karl von Piloty, a nineteenth-century German painter noted for his historical subjects.
2 Franz Xaver Winterhalter, a nineteenth-century German portrait painter.
3 François Joseph Heim, 1787-1865, a French painter.
4 Andreas Schlüter, a Baroque German sculptor.

work, that internal calm was worth more than all his inclinations of aggrandisement, and that he should resign himself to being the rich man of his kingdom, the man who can reprieve, the arbiter of small difficulties, the brilliant member, again one day the happy member of the Thousand and One Nights Club. Christian listened to him, for it was a voice of his conscience being awakened by this friend he shared feasts with, his friend, the only one on whom he could count to remain Palace Marshal in an exile, then he shook his head. "The decision has been made, the frontier camps have their orders, the dice are cast, that's the end of the conversation. Tomorrow we leave Hubert-Schloss for the great review at Gevehrstadt." And it was the keenest emotion in the Duke's life, for he saw that the features of his King were taking on a veil of decay.

The wisest of men, the most sensible, the most precise, those who only see in the way the world works the interplay of facts, occasionally have a certain fantasy, or rather, to put it more accurately, they like to take pleasure in an irregular calculation of facts, or else juggle with facts that are identical to real facts by applying them to chains of chimerical events, inferred from a possible but inexistent circumstance. This type of imaginative variation finds its outlet (when the obsessed individual is not one of the world's powerful people) in booklets about future naval battles, about the defeat of England by the French or vice versa. The specious sprayer of truth over probability is playing, in these volumes, for itself and a few matching intellectuals (perhaps they are masses and crowds) with dramas as vibrant as there possibly could be, in its audacious construction across forces, carnage, the millions and the destructions, a chance of reality; in other words leaving the cold office, where he has had multitudes of armed men cutting one another's throats, arranging them with meticulously careful imagination, and destroying them with the sudden appearance of formidable machines, whose external features he dares even to describe, a really strong and gifted power of perception of the future, finally a providence, all this entrusts him with the care of making tangible, visible and epic, the ghostly political child of his dream of the just about. Children from ten to twelve years old, as well as those who are over seventy, have often taken delight in these little imaginary wars.

In the face of these great dreams, human, mysterious or civilising, there floats, in many of the crowd's minds, this usual transmigration of facts. And whereas some dream of poems, and others of machines, some brains, and there are many of them, are obsessed with treasures discovered thanks to the magic wand of sleep, with sunken galleonsscattering from their open flanks pyramids of ingots, with castle cellars where vanquished kings forgot their war chests. How many people, on idle evenings, have ruled over Europe, or the world, or have become intoxicated on the summit of the greatest fortune, whilst others were patiently waiting for Mephistopheles whose magic power makes time, space and gravity go away for the greater pleasure of his temporary friend.

Beings frantic with practical good sense, but not exempt at some effusive times from this discharge of imagination over its counterpart, reality, did not disdain from tracing out on maps the marches of an army of which they were secretly the glorious leaders, and they would succumb to sleep just as they were entering beneath the triumphal gate, followed by horsemen in saluting ranks, flags flying, to the sound of a warrior anthem, into the capital of a powerful sovereign who was, at the same time, also sleeping, perhaps dreaming similar dreams, with a likelihood that was simply just a little greater. Mixed intellects, working in this current of ideas that some think pathological, have engraved the results of their dreams on steel; coloured geographic maps result from this, that may be considered in their number as the Epinal[1] of this mnemotechnic passion. People of an appearance that was not only correct but icy, sometimes with hairless faces, nearly always in a frock coat, have thus frequently communicated to the universe the impression of their mirage of the world, conceived in accordance with the most up-to-date of ordinary geographical maps, but turned into the slight enchantment of arabesque wandering statistics, a gentle recast of the properties of races, by excellent patriots.

---

1 Les images d'Épinal [Epinal prints] were brightly coloured prints first produced in France in the nineteenth century.

The life of King Christian had contained too many vague hours and soliloquies that he pretended he was devoting to work, for him not to have been prey to this entertainment. In his immense contemplation room, his laborious smoking room, his expanse of divans, before glass bookcases full of encyclopaedias and dictionaries, before the vast table covered with reports, extracts from reports, multiple works of all the complicated internships, how many times had he not enjoyed the pleasure of thinking about things that were perfectly senseless. The happiness of being occupied by the useless made him tremble all over, made spicier for him by a calculation of the impatience it would give to his worthy ministers, panting for a decision. Yes, King Christian, the impeccable maintainer of majorities, the expert master of commerce, the Man of the Stock Exchange, the powerful economiser, the king of business, sometimes had this lesion, and the accentuated walk of his tall body across the great park of his summer palace had often been the traumatic vehicle of a bizarre charade of facts.

Yet was it not always completely foolish if circumstances had magnificently wished to displace themselves in his desires; in any case, once the crisis was over, he would shake himself and, with his lucidity totally returned, he would whimper. But the hours spent conferring with Siegfried Gottlob, so evocative of similar wanderings in the impossible, had left him terrified of the procession of so many chimeras and, by contagion, almost an awakened sleeper. At these moments he could have been called Grand Mogul with well-established protectorates, on a new recently discovered continent, and he would have been in no way surprised, and would straight away have worked at installing his administrative services irreproachably and everywhere; the ardour of his royal Niederwaldstein cousin, the volcanic creator of projects, had won him over and it was in good faith that they had committed the one to the other, had shaken hands, had appended their signatures at the bottom of written conventions, and had lost themselves in the Atlantis of verbal promises.

The fantasy of Siegfried Gottlob: that the great sovereign of Niederwaldstein should travel, as in the classic apotheoses on the ceilings, in a miraculous chariot of clarity, victory scattering its palm fronds along his route; that, clad in the authority of a military pope over all the races of the North, he would triumph amongst the elites of vassal kings and plethora of warriors bedecked with honours and wearers of the insignia of conquest, through the largest of capitals in a place chosen by him as the ideal centre of the part of the world over which he hoped for exclusive domination. Ranks of men at arms adorning the approaches to the palaces and in the squares resonating military bands, his peoples, grateful, heads bowed and overjoyed, would see in him as he passed them by, as though through the reality of a religious vision, the ideal Victor whose gentleness heals the wounds created by his unbreakable sword; and he desired that they should be very fine, very powerful, very variegated, very rich, his cortege of allied kings, allied forever though fear and gratitude; and so he had also promised Christian the most magnificent territorial expansion.

The fantasy of Christian demanded that he should no longer be only a skilful king. His trebled possessions would increase his galas and his pomp by the same amount. The ships would leave his ports in greater triumph, and all the goods of the antipodean worlds would land on his quaysides with exultation. And since the main aim had been realised, that Hummertanz shone forth as a country of rich density and sumptuous riches in money and factory goods, it was necessary to fix on the escutcheon of the Silberglasses, the clear shade of the reflexions of military glories. The happy destiny of well-led phalanxes would rise to the temples of memory; his reputation made prouder by these high deeds, and commemorative salvoes after the death of Christian would recall anniversaries of beneficent carnage. His equestrian statues would carry at their sides a celebrated sword; and the avenues of his towns would change their peaceful names into names thundering with memories, names with epic echoes. Thus, he had accepted the promises, and potentially placed his power in the hands of the greater and more imperious strength of Siegfried Gottlob.

And the calm reflexion that followed these drills proved to him that there remained some wisdom in this temporary reduction in power, in this vassalage of King to Caesar, for in these difficult times one cannot insure crowns too much, and his was being guaranteed against internal enemies, and he was being promised expansion over the territories of his neighbours.

Christian the victorious or Christian the founder! One or the other, one would see . . .

The two monarchs, besides, were rather fond of one another. Siegfried's authoritarianism liked the smooth and crafty suppleness of Christian; Christian, very much the bureaucrat, revelled in the quick military pace of Siegfried, the prestigious speed of his disguises, the invigorating speeches, the brief proclamations in which he expended his energy. This man of action, with his calculating eyes, was like the tightrope-walker carrying out his most dangerous trick, like the acrobat in a circus (without a safety net) when the music stops, at the very moment of supreme slenderness and the most complete expenditure of energy. He was inclined to believe that crowned bureaucracies would only be saved by this bearer of the good word of the sabre, by this soldier, if he were lucky, and what is a lucky soldier? A rough young soldier that good fortune has served one evening, often because he has been the most careless; the folly of his audacity as an attacker leads him to sleep on the remains of conquered flags. In the face of the cold calculating liberals who are methodically nibbling away at Europe to shelter it (rather too much in the form of pensions) away from blows of strength and of chance, and since these liberals would, or so they said, one day be devoured by popular hunger, and would see pass by the torrent of instincts, of torches and dispossessions, salvation was there, in the last feudal properties, strong in their cohesion, and backed up by the pyrotechnics submitted too happily by the bourgeois made proud by decorations, honours, and moreover paid to do so.

This personal admiration he had for Siegfried, and this vision of things, calmed the rapid feelings of regret caused for the King of Hummertanz by the too early abandonment of his rights. Had he acted as a patriot in giving up in advance outlying parts of his territory in case there were a European war? Perhaps not, but as he thought about the future of his dynasty could he do any better? Certainly not. And, when it came down to it, Hummertanz was basically for him more a property than a fatherland. He reigned over it because his race had always been accustomed to reign, a race that was almost everywhere slightly related by marriage. For him, as for his ancestors, it was one of those Marches, one of those small Landgraviates they were given to govern over for a time, after a major war, because the great victorious powers dare not take everything. He had been chosen for Hummertanz as he might have reigned over Macedonia, if during the gracious mature years of his glorious father, they had asked for a placid sovereign for Macedonia. And then anything rather than a popular government! He had retained the most disagreeable memories of his last attempt in that domain.

His wish, the preceding year, to open the session of his Parliament in person, had delighted him. His resolve was to speak in a good-humoured way, to promise, to make more flexible the appearance of his authority, to entice by clear visions of an almost lyrical future of prosperity: railways racing headlong through expanses, diligent canals, airy schools, roads fit for carriages and bicycles, the joys of his people should want for nothing; a small amount of political freedom would one day fall from his very high munificence, in the greatest possible way! So that this would not worry him, confidant suzerain of all, but the Church and ownership which are the keystones and the charter of every country. The officials had made extravagant remarks before public opinion and had danced before the wallets of the future.

All of this could not prevent that, on his journey to the Parliament Building through the soft ranks of the town guard and the ranks of his own guard, stunned and with no precise orders about repression, the most disagreeable sounding shouts had rung out, that squares of paper bearing the grievances of the most humble common people had been thrown in handfuls at him and his staff, and that his terrified horse had wished to give the lukewarm servants of his power, and the most hostile squawkers, the lamentable spectacle of an unhorsed Majesty.

It was therefore faithful to his dynasty, to his institution as a King, to his responsibility to those of his that would come in the future, and to his solidarity with those in the past, that he was incorporating himself in the powerful league of kings in order to defend and to impose a moderate absolutism, and almost serenely, that he went to the great military review of Gevehrstadt, given in his honour, the official sign of the new alliance.

III

ON ordinary days, the exercise ground extended its flat horror as far as the small green and silent hillslopes, at the bottom of which the small low shacks of the targets were upholding their severity; groups of men lost in this blank expanse were exhausting themselves, were huffing and puffing, were galloping, running, kneeling, standing up again; close to the hillsides, despite their sad greenery that was almost black, there was not the gaiety but at least the share of living noise attributed to this military site; mobile canteens were popping up for a moment, the crisp detonations of firearms were creating variety against the racket of the schools of buglers and of fifes and drums, whose discordant exercises were carried far away by the wind, to terrorise one's ears. On to this terrain, urgent horsemen were arriving, arrogant in their advance, morally and physically rigid; at their approach the small groups were squeezing together, and were becoming petrified, rigid, the movements were crisper, the shouts more piercing, and the first horsemen to arrive were soon off to meet the new arrivals, crisp as well; having been spectators they were now becoming an integral part of the spectacle; and early on, this whole space would empty itself, abandoned, made even vaguer by the monotonous drive of a few invalids, the capers of brats in tattered clothes, and the rival and fraternal frolics to those of this group of children of a considerable population of dogs. The afternoon concerts, without the charm of the morning ones, at least had variety and it was anger, plaintive cries and scandal if, by chance, a whim had the troops once again occupying this terrain which, in deed if not by right, should belong to the rather noisy contemplatives that compose the children and the rigmaroles in the capitals.

On special days it was clearly not possible to diminish the brackish ugliness of this stretch of land; the addition of a few grandstands, simple woodworks, do not brighten it up. But one was relying on the splendour of the uniforms, and on the arrival of the happy crowd of Gevehrstadtians, with their ordinary cortege of small shopkeepers armed with wheelbarrows, hawker's trays or caravans. They were all running, the petit bourgeois eager for their walk, the chauvinistic clerks who like to match their pace to that of the army, the untidy slackers in their flat caps and really old frock coats, and the fat brewers, and the sickly thin employees of the little luxury industries. From the elegant alleys that could just about be seen in the distance towards the city, there emerged, bedecked with flowers, landaus cradling beauties that were made gently nonchalant amongst the blooms, beside upright functionaries with a star around their necks, or unattached soldiers, more upright, their trunks straighter even though they were sitting down, than those that were about to parade. The fat bankers were arriving as well, their faces pink or red above their grey chinstrap beards; in comfortable carriages they were coming to be present at the passing by of the bayonets that were protecting society and its interests; and behind them the money changers were coming in their cabs, and behind them was arriving the army of those kept busy by cash boxes and the fateful errands of money collection, and that day many socialist colloquia were breaking up for their most joyful members, thoughtless proletarians, were making their way hastily towards this free spectacle.

Apart from a few privileged ones, the heroes of the spectacle had had to come quite a few kilometres in order to show their splendour to the interested onlookers. Their chinstraps with coloured plumes revealed sweating faces. The extraordinary banality communicated to a wall of men the perfect identity of shapes, colours, metallic gleams, made their number seem smaller. The officers on horseback paraded past them like gigantic vegetables growing in regular rows in a field; to the side, the masses of the cavalry, more lustrous, recalled the mediaeval appearance of the country and of its Crown. Helmets with formidable visors and enormous neck-protectors coquettishly upturned at the edge, breastplates decorated with relief images of terrible birds, sword blades with pennons, the multiplicity of brasses and steels, provided the rigidity of this enormous crowd with the appearance of a huge force, of a mastiff ready and formidably armed.

And there were contrasts, the simplicity of the shapes of the canons, the very modern complexities of the horse teams proved that the human tool, amassed here, could be flexible or rigid, giving the idea of the great undermining of men. Also the diverse movements, the slow and comical pyrrhic dance of modern parades aroused enthusiasm, and the whole of Gevehrstadt beat with an immense unison, where there was aesthetics, chauvinism, security, good cheer, the gentle sensation of the race course, mixed with blisters inflicted on the meninges by the twists and turns of melodrama, when this army passed by before kings and so many lofty barons. The latter were bursting with colours and sparkling with gemstones. The nickels of the saddles and the materials of the shabracks, the gaudy ribbons on their chests, the gilded floating of their capes, the variegated bellies, the tumultuous sashes, the helmets of pure metal, their cockerel's tail feathers and painted manes, the plumes on their shakos and colbacks, were bejewelling the space, the undulating blur of army; to the right and to the left stretched the jumble of the bright female outfits and the stiff stature of the valets.

Christian was experiencing joy like the others, as he saw the steady gait of the defenders, the clustering of the people to be subdued and the interlacing of the officers climbing gradually towards Caesar. He was not unaware that the old feudal instinct had largely been replaced by a hierarchy, below a paternal despotism, capable of hiding trifling matters, paying urgent debts, energetically protecting his man at arms from those wielders of legal paperwork; but the link was nevertheless perhaps even stronger.

So he gave hearty commendations, when with the troops mingling on the horizon towards their lines of retreat, the crowd grouped around the confines of the exercise ground in order to acclaim their passage, the escorts of the leaders remained alone near the little target house. Siegfried Gottlob had gathered his guests and his officers for a toast and pronounced the following little speech; he had already often revised it.

"The manoeuvres of today have proved to us, once more, the cohesion and the agreement of all the parts of the army, they are a proof of the devotion of all our subjects and allies at the very point where they have been placed by Destiny, the symbol of the wishes of God from whom we hold our power. This agreement of all, in a desired submission and an initiative skilfully put to our service, teaches us that the army is ready to combat any external enemy that tried to disaggregate the work of our illustrious ancestors, and also any internal one if evil days, as some lost voices of prophets threaten us, should come again, the sinister echo of times past, the honour and the discipline of our army, that is the holy glory of the fatherland, would be able to overcome them."

IV

BUT in the evening grave news arrived to trouble King Christian who was conjuring up his butterflies of hope by rocking himself to the tune of some vague occasional music, composed for this gala evening. How far away she is, the white image of the dancer, and the mirrors of desire held out to him by the bent arms of his lady friends, and far away the bow of Diana that she has wielded in such a mutinous manner. The first news that Sparkling has gleaned was saddening but not terrifying. The big docks of Geldwachs where are piled up the drums of petroleum, the demijohns of alcohol, the jars of oil, the barrels of petrol, the sheds housing oils from Tehran and Pennsylvania, the paraffins, are on fire, and against the grey sky of the sea with its barges, the red horror of an Antaeus-like fire, replenishing its strength from the flaming earth; despite the prodigious help of everyone, the fire has reached the small, yellow, pitiful district, where with great pints of beer the sailors calm the diverse nostalgic memories they have of their beaches of origin.

One is vaguely aware that the terror of this fire, suddenly deflagrating amongst these hovels, already overwhelmed with drunken sleep and sleazy friendships, has caused rackets and affrays, paralysing the helpers through the multiplicity of shouts; and the inhabitants of the peaceful districts of Geldwachs only think of isolating their dwellings from the lip of the volcano. The Inferno is running riot with a masterful strength, as a fire of Fate coming to destroy the docks, the banks and the counters; and explosions are sizzling as it makes its progress with ragged wings like enormous hands with multiple pointing fingers. It is the explosion of piles of cartridges bought cheaply, so as to extract from them gunpowder and lead to be sent to gullible negroes; it is the larva coming from the cellars of the houses already consumed and licking the bases of the houses not yet on fire. All the scientific assemblages of materials, all the resources of prudence, all the forces for the expectations of price rises, all the skills, all the examples of genius, the cunning traditions that were transmitted in this city, which were a secure inheritance and a labyrinth thread for life, all this only made the catastrophe worse. And here on the horizon are flaming like a bright fire the immense stocks of Norwegian wood, and giant salamanders are rejoicing for a minute as their hidden life bursts out in the terrible brightness; and beneath the deeper light, the pale faces and the movements of the bodies are puny appearances of useless and desperate silhouettes. The duty was simple, it was imperative to leave the next day for Geldwachs.

But the next day there tolled another knell, just as sinister, just as concrete.

When a new nation, with little cash at its disposal but on the other hand rich in arable land, in useful minerals, wants to exchange a part of its resources and its hopes against ready money, it encounters the financier, perhaps not Turcaret[1] but rather more similar to those Harpagons[2] who preferred not to give in exchange genuine promises but rather plaintive mandolins and declimatised saurians. Obviously the form was modified but it is no less true that in exchange for a rather limited amount of gold, the borrowing country commits a great amount of its future resources and that it contracts obligations; the obliging European who had to take so much trouble (he sweats just thinking about it) to sound the stampede (or rather to bring together a syndicate of brave lynxes) asks little for himself; a reasonable affluence will crown the enhancement, already too late, of a country he loves, whose development he is following with a peerless interest, which was for a long time the basis of his best estimates about the market of universal wealth. But it is not on his own that he has been able to bring together great sums of money, the formidable piles of consolation that one wanted, in fine living gold, he adds pleasantly, in exchange for securities, and securities are not, whatever one might

---

1 The main character in a comedy of that name, about a financier, by Lesage, first performed in 1709.
2 Harpagon is the central character in Moliere's comedy of 1668 *L'Avare*.

say, money. And so commissions have to be paid and monopolies handed out; all the banks have to be satisfied, all the omens have to be paid so that the hesitant crowd listens to the charlatan's patter and stops over it, and so that this scattered money is brought together for the greatest good of countries like Guatemala.

At this point there arrive in the new nation those responsible for monopolies and concessions; for every effort they make, really for their own profit, they will ask for benefits, on the pretence of general interest and upon pain of upsetting Europe of which they represent the serious elite; the subsidies they are given, the new lines of credit signed to them, these are as nothing; the wealth of the provinces is assured by the gigantic railway lines that they erect like a bridge from the Savannah to the Pampas. Besides, are they not aware in the Guatemalas of this world that the courteous but tenacious representative of the bearers of European securities is in no way exaggerating his credit with the leaders of his nation. Even if the number of his friends associated with his fortune was small, if they were only three to possess the fifty or five hundred thousand papers ratified by the debtor State, they would be no less, in the eyes of the powers always looking for the rich friend and the great coloniser with large hands, fifty or five hundred thousand poor people, plagued and worried, if not harmed. And the debtor State yields, and the burden of charges, the back interest increases just as the quantity of goods available to be committed decreases.

But it happens, on the other hand, that new men in the Guatemalas get the people to understand what degree of exploitation is imposed on them. The latter insinuate that in all contracts no one has clean hands; they open their eyes to the following point, that legality is possibly not absolutely the law; that if the preceding regime has accepted obligations that are ruining their land for a long time, that are impoverishing them, as well as raising the cost of living, it is permissible for them to return to the past, to re-examine their affairs, and in future to pay for the service they receive just the going rate, without moreover trying to recuperate anything from the years when these services were over-priced.

However it happens at this moment that many people find themselves unjustly robbed by these decisions for they too have listened to the mendacious voice of the banks, and have accepted to pay for the Guatemala bonds the price they would have been worth if everything had remained in its prosperous state; these people are now ruined.

It happens that the banks have not been able entirely to relinquish all these papers, and in fact kept in reserve a large quantity of them for fraudulent operations. Their wealth decreases with each fall in the fictitious value of their securities; their deposits, committed as collateral against this fictitious value, go down the drain and poor people lose their small investments. The misery becomes greater and for the privileged unease is seen.

The result of this tangle of financial matters, the struggle between the former robbed person and his robber, who has already partly and fruitfully disposed of his gain, is called a financial crash.

Guatemala had caused a crash and Geldwachs was, more than any other city, financially involved in the crash, and King Christian was the most significant amongst the managers of gold in Geldwachs.

PERPETUAL ERYNNIES[1]

---
1 Furies.

I

ALONG the well-dressed avenues of a modern city, totally white with gold lettering on the balconies, close to thin trees still garlanded with the withered remains of the recent feast, a little dry old man, anachronistically rigged out in a lapis-lazuli riding coat, with hair *à la financière*[1] and long side-tresses, is capering with small, short movements; his crafty eyes are laughing in his clean-shaven face; his footsteps hobble along coquettishly like a trill of a dancing melody, his hand is holding a bouquet of cornflowers and anemones. The genuine citizens, their heads informally covered with dome-shaped black cylinders or metal helmets, are gazing at him more amused than surprised and it would be a puerile and amusing evocation without the too exuberant and noisy joy of the urchins; but here is proceeding towards him, just as outdated, her dress decorated with flowers and farthingales, like a spring scene on a Chinese plate, a courteous dowager under this awakened sky, despite the jerkiness of her

---

1 A sort of ponytail.

small precise footsteps; a meeting and coquettish and light-hearted greetings, hand-kissing, and the couple sets off festively as if they are following the steps of invisible strolling fiddlers; but suddenly their footsteps stumble, a filthy carriage has run them over in its brutal dash, people scurry and the gaiety of those present dressed in frock-coats and jackets takes on a tinge of sadness as though some precious toy has just been destroyed; a feeling of regret encompasses the passers-by as if some tiny herald has just shouted out that the great Pan of dolls is definitely broken.

King Christian woke from this dream in something of a cold sweat. The carriage that had waited for his secret return to Krebsbourg was arriving at the Palace, and the cold dawn of the morning was bathing the motionless gardens in blue air. Christian wished to try to rest for a few hours before consulting with his ministers about the serious situations that were happening.

Ah, this dream was well and truly the allegory of what was going to happen! These amiable figurines of the past were evoking the whole idea of false happiness, the superficial elegance that adorns the nonchalant and rich and festive life of the small country in a Europe pregnant with a painful future. This brutal shock which ruffled so much the pock-marked buffoons, did it not conjure up the sudden outpouring, in unexpected crossroads, of great forces that are never tamed, that one is impotent to keep dozy for long, and who whimpering for a long time in a fearful sleepwalk, appear on a day of total rumpus in the formidable noise of giant rattles, in tumultuous excitement. That is when by the light of flaming torches, during terrible hours when the small out-dated and unfashionable monarchies which still sketch out ghostly minuets, on memories of ancient ariettas, fall at the shock of knocks at the door and the detonations of hunting rifles that are, on this day, weapons of war.

II

BENEATH the hammer blows of misfortune Hummertanz was thinking very severely about its dynasty. The admirable theory of the scapegoat appeals to the masses; to them it seems logical that the Head of State personally expiates the calamities raining down on the country. Aristocracies, parliamentary powers, the people normally designate them by a symbolic "They. . ."pronounced more often than not with rancour, with the bitter tone that encompasses an infinite chain of persecutors, starting with the foreman and ending with sovereigns. Recently, "They. . ." was truly considered with ever-increasing contempt. Nothing was working, wages were going down, towns were burning, the crash had just locked down the banks and extinguished the factory furnaces. These days, the common people left to their own devices by the anxieties of the capitalists, had all the time in the world to hold meetings, to create little parliaments in all the cafés, to exacerbate with toxic alcohols its hatreds and its demands and to refine them. "They" quickly became the sovereign. Myths with giant wings set forth launched by thousands of secret meetings, embellishing themselves in every corner of the province with a dash of local wit.

And over Krebsbourg it was like a cloud of annoying rumours, like flights of accusatory dervishes whirling over the houses, launching germs of sedition over all the hovels of the poor districts. Great strikes were declared and the black country, the country of coal and iron filled the trains with numerous delegations of concentrated and taciturn crowds who were coming to the capital to ask for more bread, more rights, the better era, and were thinking of snatching power from unworthy hands, to set off towards a new experience, and who knows, perhaps a happier one, for hope endlessly weaves muslins of glory and luminous materials that it waves in front of the crowds, whilst always taking one step back away from them.

King Christian was resolved to defend himself. The catastrophe of Geldwachs had embittered him, had damaged his fortune. The rumours, basically true, that were circulating about his rapacity, his treasures, his prudent and marvellous investments in secure countries, were hounding him. The liberals attacked him for having left hanging over his country the threat of a foreign invasion; they had guessed the role of the camps filled with Niederwaldsteinian troops. Everyone was searching for who would be the foreigner whose entry would be the most to their liking since the country was clearly open. The elites were seized by fear in the face of this unknown, the invasion and its consequences: more rigid power, or perhaps the enemy settling down under various pretexts, and perhaps annexation. The clergy, not consulted in this instance, were muttering; and the powerless deacons, the whole mass of the chaplains of small parishes were in agitation, dreaming of a beneficent theocracy, of a reign of the ministers of Christ, summoning to the universal Last Supper, flocks to whom their hands would every day distribute their share of material and moral happiness. In the face of the attacks in the press, unexpected disclosure of many tribunes, haranguing small groups at all the corners of the capital, the powers that be brought forth from their arsenals an old law of lese-majesty applying to criticism of present times the penalties applicable to personal outrages towards the King; and there were unfortunately as a result numerous arrests; it was to extract its mentors from their prison that the people rose up.

III

THE considerable buildings of the law court and the prison dominate the highest hilltop in Krebsbourg. The law court has its foundations deep in the sad alleyways of ill repute; the presence here, in earlier times, of a calvary results in all the threads of bricks bearing the more gentle and more expressive names of the Passion; here and there, when the hill flattens out for a few metres and the street gets wider, there are shabby markets where can be bought everything that has kept any value. The architecture of the law court is cold but comfortable; nowhere is official grey diffused over more monotonous building blocks. Its general shape recalls, in a scholarly assemblage, all the earlier courts of tyranny, its internal halls are allegories of immense railway stations, enormous waiting rooms for penitentiary countries. Not a single internal ornament diminishes the severe rigidity of this verdict-hive; on the facade a few statues, those of ephemeral promises of justice, equality, protection, which accentuate the ironical aspect of this temple of judgment. Quite naturally the prison deferred in beauty to its hierarchical superior, the law court; on the edge of this hilltop, visible from afar to pedestrians and to prison warders making their way towards Krebsbourg, it scattered huge piles of pink bricks beneath an enormous cupola that bay windows dressed up as a cage; around, wasteland, occasionally sown with a small amount of market gardening, where the prison warders on their hours off could devote themselves to their taste for gardening, which, along with that of raising little birds shines forth so delightfully in the least sombre corners of the human soul; further away, a few leprous hovels, sleazy watering holes, are spaced out. The earth of this scrofulous spot is as though stricken by sterility, and fatal prey for the rubble collectors. It was towards these two buildings that there wished to advance the columns of the crowd aiming to destroy and set free.

The laws, the constitution of Hummertanz armed its bourgeoisie with considerable power. The bourgeoisie had really taken the place of the aristocracy, its defunct elder sister. Mistress of *determinative* power, through the absolute right of the ballot paper, proportionate in number to the well-established figures of unearned income, mistress of the executives of the future since it alone was able to nourish its children with knowledge to turn them into colonels, engineers and judges, the bourgeoisie had also inherited the prerogative to bear arms, at least once a week, and in public. Despite the relative rarity of this military evocation, the notables nevertheless had, at home, at the discretion of and for the service of the State, sabres, rifles and cartridges. The axiom was that those with possessions protect the

State against those without possessions. A sagacious measure had further refined these dispositions, allocating the richest factory owners or proprietors to the cavalry squadrons, so that the high and low bourgeoisie were duly distinct and indicated by an external emblem visible to all. These benefits never fail to charm the heart of a group of the privileged. Nevertheless, on these days, the bourgeoisie was grumbling since the Crash had largely bent its tall stems and the full ears of wheat of the annual harvest had been declared empty. As a result, the cavalry was feeling a sort of alienation for a dynasty whose forecasts and assessments seemed infirm, almost insane; but the infantry, for the most part, more solidly attached by its operations to the intangible and inalienable loan to the State, retained its solidity and its faith in their entirety. It would certainly, by the tenor of its devotion, drag in the squadrons, whose captains should basically realise that a few defeats are not total ruin, and that to prevent total ruin, the best and least expensive of means was to charge, by all the noble principles they inherited. Thus when, in provincial city streets, ill-disciplined bands of the unemployed were threatening to use against the powers that be all the tiny armaments that can be appropriated from ordinary life, such as iron circles from the foot of trees, revolvers, metal knuckle-dusters, etc. . . ., they would encounter serious and serene lines, fortified by excellent carbines. The bourgeois guard raised itself up to be truly the talisman of the establishment. It was much more reliable than the army: for the recruitment of the latter consisted of paid volunteers, of military substitutes, of a lot of lazy scoundrels from the fields and small-time districts; their war-like instincts were nil, and so one had to rely on their innate feeling for combat and their love of uproar, on their habits of fighting and looting in cafés, on their reliable erudition where methodical destruction is concerned, meticulously angry, which breaks and sullies everything, capable of making cold inventories of the devastated houses, to make sure that nothing has been left intact. The plan of the military councils held by the general staff and the civil ministers, who for so long had been aware of and were manipulating opinion, was to use as far as possible the army against the working-class centres. They were speculating on the muted hatred which separates the worker from the soldier, a hatred nurtured by fights in taverns, of the disdain of the soldier with his fine decorative uniform for the rags of the proletarian, and also the contempt of the proletarian for the bailiff's man he thinks of as an idler, and to whom he frequently gives the epithets slacker or lazy bones.

 The victors on this day in Krebsbourg have, as is often the case, tarted up their bloody triumph by using the whole presumed ignominy of the attacking masses. These few people, the twenty men who were almost all young unimportant students, were they worth having dead bodies bearing witness to a useless affection for them. Was it not a curious mistake about the intentions of the Law to believe that they were exposed to barbaric punishments, to illegal executions? Only a hollow mind, like that of Papegay-Garten, could not only convince himself, but voice it loudly, trumpet it, riot again against it. The only true means of attracting grace to these malevolent leaders, preserved within strong fortified walls, was that their friends should be quiet and wait. The law, in its majesty, does not wish to be defied. If one waits for the sentence to arise from the river of life and wisdom that the law has symbolised through the ungrateful ages of the struggle for life, its fair scales of justice indicate from the closest at hand true innocence or irrefutable guilt. After the word has been uttered in the guaranteed Silences of the praetorium, bolstered by all pressures from above or below, by its irrefutable contract with the loyal Executive, one may wait for the word clemency, which never, in less troubled times, leaves its pacifying manna wanting; for, if the judge is inflexible, the King is paternal. The judge guides the hesitant conscience of the sovereign towards the choice of truth, but once this task is complete, he leaves the King to spare his cities the horror of executions and to dispense human pardon. The guilty impatience of the demagogues was the only casual force which stretched out along the streets those who were marching and were too proud of their mistakes. Ah, if they had known, before the hours of grief, how to soften their grudges of dissatisfied ambitious men, and in a fleeting moment of lucidity how to preach calm, peace, disarmament to this crowd that was saturated with their teachings, how many evils could have been spared! The statue of the State nevertheless continued to stand tall, and the floods of anger and horror smashed against its granite plinth; but at what price. And the stern powers of the law and of duty, once the job was complete, and the struggle was over, cannot help being troubled, nor shedding a tear, thinking of all these lives taken away from useful jobs, of these arms lost for work, for production, for overproduction, for colonisation and for the most painful although necessary and providential land clearances.

The flawed voice of those who had boosted the riot, who were now sheltered from just prosecutions by the toleration of countries like Switzerland and America, may thunder with cursing, or seduce by the specious nature of their arguments. And the fact that they were safe and sound on the very evening of this butchery, and their easy escape from the country where they were toxic, does this not incriminate their shouts for reprisals and the grunting discords of their false unhappiness? Then, is it certain, as they claim, that so many obscure heroes, civic patriots, humble oblates of the pure religion of solidarity had bullet holes in them.

With the regrettable and fatal exception of a few who went astray, that the pernicious doctrines of these men sacrificed by striking them against the unconscious rigidity of necessary punishment, their soldiers of disorder, their clonic vagabonds with menacing hands, were they able to extirpate them from the dregs of cities, amongst those that the common law has withered in the discordant slime of inveterate vices; from what despised mass graves arises the riot with its twisted claws? And many other similar arguments were found in the statements of the right-minded press on the days following scuffles.

It will be of no use proving to the masters of authority the slender value of the arguments they are deploying here, to maintain that if the riot had triumphed, the next day the country would have been happier and better governed; neither the casts nor the historians in their pay care for truth, but only for arguments to establish the relevance of their acts.

IV

THE MINISTER FOR WAR, Count Imerstetten, was endowed with an excellent military reputation. His service record was fine although peaceful because for a long period the sabres of Hummertanz had remained hanging in the cloakrooms. Previously, thanks to a gracious leave of absence, he had been able to devote himself to the service of the Pope, the temporal sovereign.

The total lack of skirmishes at that time had allowed him to acquire the reputation as an excellent guards' officer. The good relations he had been able to develop in the capital of Catholicism helped him to visit many other capital cities as a military attaché; his perspicacious eye followed many manoeuvres, and his competence where military dress and weaponry was concerned was cited. The creation of an admirable dolman[1] led him to glory; the press was haunted by his name. His genuine skill as a horseman, and his deep friendships with the bishops and prelates marked him

---

1 A type of military uniform.

out, no longer to follow, but to be in command of the manoeuvres of the Hummertanz armies. He smartened up the campaign uniform, modified the water bottle, thinned down the rifle strap, succeeded in having the marching songs of the soldiers, hitherto rather cynical, replaced by pretty cantilenas that had been expressly composed and that were urgently holier-than-thou. But what put the seal on his reputation, were his reports about manoeuvres! It was he who declared following one of these well-organised excursions that such and such a regiment had taken such and such a village with the most boiling hot courage, and that Major X***had defended the bridge at ***down to his very last cartridge. He was thus, given his ignorance about ballistics and camp building, and the truly vibrant aspects of his character, the ideal army chief.

This day's riot was his first battle. King Christian had called him in confidentially, and had soberly warned him that were there to be a defeat for the forces of order, the friend from Niederwaldstein would really come to lend a hand and that it was better to sort it out oneself. For the fatherland and for his military reputation, the general decided to repress everything to perfection: humanity is the finest jewel in our moral crown, but victory is the aim of the armed soldier.

Therefore, following the theories and experiences of the most fashionable victors, he sketched out an irreproachable battle plan which allowed him, with his unbreakable centre protecting the Palaces, the Banks, the prison and a few pleasure gardens (by a stroke of good fortune the Museums were close to the Palaces), to be able to turn his flanks on the flood of protestors; besides, a cunning diversion via the poor districts would allow him to attack them from behind. Once this repression had been carried out, the general was counting on using for their final destruction the bones and craniums of the bourgeois guard who had here the most illuminous interests, and to entrust to it the guard of the well-dredged city, and to be able to dispose his regular units to take the good word out to the provinces. Victory would quickly come thanks to his system of allowing the revolutionaries to arm themselves quietly (what would they find) in their poverty-stricken streets and even to pillage a few gunsmiths, and then to crush them in one go. His calculation succeeded; the populace armed itself, crossed the districts of the city centre, given over to small shops, acting like kids, bending the iron shop fronts, smashing a few windows. As they were closer to the army, they were irritated by feints of police jostling; a tiny cavalry charge elicited shots from their mob and so battle was engaged.

One could never have presaged so much solidity from the cloth and silk trades, for the enthusiasm for fire of those in the wings. Was it for the most part the grocery or the jewellery trade which counted heroes amongst these men so fond of the bayonet? A difficult proportion to establish! Difficult tactics, formations of platoons on the thresholds of churches, to strike down with bullets the rebels trapped in the choir, these were carried out with the same precision as if they were manoeuvres. The vanquished poor people, accused of setting houses on fire by feeding the flames with petrol, were shot by devoted squads; nothing carried on for very long.

For a long time, Christian, terrified, distressed by so much blood, has been increasing his efforts to stop the firing. Sparkling, not listened to the previous day, suspect despite his loyalty and his firm decision to fight for the royal prerogative, is proving to the King that things are going too far, that with some calm, a few isolated acts of force were enough to provoke a rout in this crowd that was now exasperated and defending itself with all the arms it possessed; and still he is not able to convince him quickly, for hesitant, terrified, Christian on horseback in the large square that has been cleared, surrounded by his staff, is listening to other voices and other opinions; he follows the forward march of his troops, weeps at places where blood has been shed, finally orders the cease fire. But how to have one's order obeyed? As soon as firing has stopped at one point, it crackles out again in another, by mistake. Then nothing can be prevented any longer. The bourgeois guard is bitterly taking revenge for its fears, is drawing punishment from the thousand tribulations inflicted on it every day by the working class. The sombre Bellona[1] of civil wars is floating over the houses with their sashes of fire, for the population is setting buildings on fire to cover its retreat and is barring, through this incandescent destruction, the path against its fierce pursuers. Nothing can be stopped any more.

Prince Otto, Christian's second son, heir presumptive since the death of Prince Max-Eric, is involved as

---

1 An ancient Roman goddess of war.

an officer in the movement to encircle the riot. The cohort, encouraged by his presence, converges on the last defensive position of the wretches. These are the huge markets leading down to the canals. The most energetic and best armed of the revolutionaries continue the struggle to allow the women and children, who are not spared from the shots and the salvoes of fire, and the wounded and the weakest and the least bold, to escape onto the numerous barges tied up at the quayside. A few houses, a few barricades linking iron buildings with shutters creating safe firing points, give them the simulacrum of a fortress, and in spite of the terrible attack from the troops who have finally been engaged, fractious and exasperated by the odour of gunpowder and blood, whilst the bourgeois guards wipe their brows covered with sweat, they resist for a time, but only for a short time, for the great detonations of the artillery are multiplying in frequency and in convergent death; and then the cavalry has managed, in other places, to reach the bank of the canal that is already full of boats into which too many people are crowded and the hussars cut the haulers down with sabres, and canons sink the barges, whilst the resistance in the markets has just died, in all the corners, all the cellars, on all the flat parts of the little alleys, and fire is taking over this last citadel of the libertarians.

The King was going back up towards his palace, overwhelmed, followed by his aides-de-camp; on the Main Square, the Minister for War, the victor, brought him his son, Prince Otto, who had, or so said the general, covered himself in glory and on whom a slight wound gave the definitive sign of a warrior. Christian could scarcely utter his thanks and his promises of order, advancement, etc. . . . The words of his short speech to the officers stuck in his throat. His gratitude passed through swollen lips. It was a man who had aged by twenty years who was replying to the salutes of the buglers of the troops dispersed on guard duty around the major junctions, to keep watch on any eventuality, and to the acclamations of the bourgeois guards whose dispersal was taking place with some difficulty, as they picked off specks around the improvised inns. The King went back into the palace gloomy and in pieces. He was saddened by all the willingness to congratulate him.

Indeed, they were soon all gathered together there, the mitred abbots, the gaudy ones, the diplomats, the finest flowers of the elite, the accredited representatives of royal cousins, those responsible for dossiers in the pasty white buildings of ministries, the egg-shaped craniums of the heads of credit companies, those with a large annuity with their statesman-like side-whiskers and with perfect partings in their hair. The black jackets with modest stars were bowing down before purple capes. And he who judges that his soul necessitates an external appearance like that of Mr. Gladstone is rubbing shoulders with the man whose moustache is like that of Humbert.[1] This stubborn customs functionary who sees himself as the spitting image of Bismarck is conversing with the shady, officious journalist who is

---

1 King Humbert I of Italy known for his splendid moustache.

trying to look like Crispi.¹ Bilious sallow men, with their opera hats under their arms, are congratulating the brilliant dragoon, with his bushy beard like that of an Eisenfahrt. The simiesque snobbishness is bowing down before large possessions. The notaries are massaging the hands of the magistrates in a manner that is more clammy, more smooth, more affirmative, more supportive than ever; humble functionaries turned a little green, turning a little yellow with this dazzling glory of the truculent soldiers, are expressing mealy-mouthed congratulations. And soon here is the brilliant swarm of the ladies: "The circumstances are sad; what will the gracious Queen say? What a painful surprise at the Château de Thieve! What does she know about it? Has she already received the comforting news? She will be very distressed as she is the patroness of the poor; and yet she will be proud of Prince Otto!"

But the King was so perfectly sad, responded so languidly that soon there came about a movement into the large salon with the portraits of ancestors and so Christian found himself for a moment alone with Sparkling, also distressed, and two or three friends, chamberlains and hunters, confidants of great summer outings, saddened by his grief, whilst high society, weeping, formed a large circle around the young Prince and heir, whose marvellous conduct the General did not cease to recount to all. The day seemed to have deposed Christian, the down-payment on a future reign of force was being paid.

---

1 Francesco Crispi, a nineteenth-century Italian Prime Minister.

※

At this moment, near the corner of the monumental fireplace where those who are already of the past are gathering, Sparkling's adjutant is standing, rigidly, saluting militarily, but with such a worried expression that it is clear that something serious has happened. Sparkling walks towards him and immediately appears so terrified that the King and his friends draw close. What has happened? "The private apartments of the King and Queen have been broken into," and the adjutant, having posted a guard and not daring himself to take stock of the only too clear disaster, comes to refer the matter to the Marshal. And the King wished to accompany Sparkling. A cursory investigation showed them opened safes, desks smashed open with mallets, empty caskets thrown on the carpets. The theft was serious for the Queen's admirable jewel collection, and the diamonds, of which the King had a marvellous selection, all these were missing, and unremitting hammers had broken the precious frames of miniatures. And as Sparkling, in the face of the increasingly distraught sadness of the King, tries a few words of consolation, for the thieves were bound to be caught, Christian says to him: "Dear friend, this is perhaps the last blow: we have been wrong all the time recently and in the past; today we have fired for no reason, for less than no reason, for the person who came here to steal is no doubt in no way the ally of those we have been obliged to conquer with this useless butchery. Just think, Sparkling, the Palace and all the adjacent buildings were too strongly defended for even one of the rioters to get in; and it is my opinion, whatever your colleagues the ministers are saying, that the lure of filthy lucre was not the thing that attracted the poor to the red flags and black flags. There is something rotten in Hummertanz, Sparkling, beneath the ecclesiastical stole and beneath the uniform, and beneath all the medals. Who can be accused? No doubt someone from our circle. Who has stolen the goods belonging to someone else? But no doubt some pious fellow recommended by our bishops, well known to the beings who frequent our numerous corridors, some slippery agent of our bank chiefs, perhaps one of the chiefs themselves, for, do not forget, my friend, that they blame me for the Crash; perhaps he wanted to recuperate his losses from the principal culprit?"

"It is exactly, Sire, what our unfortunates of this morning wished to do against them; they call it, I believe, individual recovery; without in any way conceding the truth of that view, I find that this way of thinking is very widespread. Sire, it seems to me that our monarchy is disappearing since the nobles have allowed themselves to be so closely allied to the bankers . . . to be in their pockets; but, since the adjutant has, as soon as he knew about this abduction of property, had the doors of the palace sealed, would you allow us to search ourselves to see if we cannot find something, some clue?"

"All right, my dear Sparkling, but let us not talk any more about it. I would be afraid, during a hypocritical expression of sympathy, to notice in the eyes of one of my faithful followers already a hint of remorse. . . Ah! What a setback, Sparkling, I had a son, a son that I loved, as you know; valour and skill could be seen on his hot-headed forehead, he would have been . . . But those men, for want of any activity worthy of them, expend their energy in murderous nonsense; I have another son, my whole consolation as I saw him grow up, tire out ponies, play at soldiers and learn lessons throughout his life, was that he was not the elder and that he would not reign; and now, for a splinter of wood in his hand, he is no less proud than Tamburlaine the Great; as for me, all I risked was to impoverish Hummertanz. What will he do for it, where will my wife, the Queen, spend her last years when she has been dispossessed? Just another victim for the Museum in London that collects outdated sovereigns, cyclical and reactivated."

One of the chamberlains was joining them and, hearing the last words, was trying to distract the King. And Christian replied: "One is always too late to see clearly, the best see clearly the minute after the one that demanded a quick decision, and in that case what matters the difference between the intelligent and the stupid man, since everything is irreparable. Come on, let us look at the servants' wings, perhaps we fill find out something there."

Corridors, walkways, staircases, glazed rotundas with leather divans, then again, more series of chambers, all closed, in corridors, the overwhelming silence of a deserted place. They were at a sort of bay window looking out over the city. A singular laziness of the magistrature had allowed to remain there, right opposite the outbuildings of the Palace, houses of ill repute, hotels with a bad reputation. Who had taken refuge there? Perhaps it was thought that a few Palace servants used to come to look ironically at these ruins from behind the window pane; who carried out the act, nothing was ever known, still nothing is known. But the terrible detonation of a bomb exploded in the room where Christian was standing; two of the chamberlains were lying on the ground, Sparkling was unhurt; at the noise of the explosion doors opened, the little rotunda was instantly full. Christian, leaning against a wall, was meticulously brushing with his hand a flap of his tunic, the reflections of a fire still burning turned the windows pink, he tried to smile. Sparkling, who had hurried towards him, saw that the King was no longer aware of anything; he took him away in his arms and soon Christian, stretched out on his bed, was murmuring a nursery rhyme in a broken voice, was signalling that people should be quiet, seemed to be listening to a far-off din, then started purring again whilst Sparkling was convulsively twisting his moustache.

V

THE decision of Prince Otto, who had been immediately appointed Prince Regent (except that this would need to be ratified the next day by parliamentary acts), was that King Christian should be taken to the Château de Thieve. It was hoped that the sight of the Queen . . . or perhaps really nothing was hoped other than proceeding to new business in a more tranquil way. Moreover the countryside there was becoming agitated; the presence of the King, who had become such a moving person, would perhaps be a reassurance for these people in the far off heathlands; perhaps the gentle madness of King Christian would give to these simple folk the legendary appearance of a dolorous saint struck down one day, for the sins of his people, by the hand of providence, and a special train took away from Krebsbourg the King, Sparkling, henceforth his guard for life, destined to mirror himself to the end in this terrible blackness of existence, plus an escort. In truth, the Marshal was not at all appalled by this exile from the new court and this new care, his thankless and desolate task. He would find in the bleak dialogue with the old child, in an existence full of alarms of a hospitaller, the serious punishment which seemed to him to be the just and grave end of a life of a light-headed witty man, and he looked forward to listening to his soul in the silence. Crushed, the King was sleeping as the royal train raced without stopping through stations shaking their windows like peals of thunder, climbing hills, going down into ravines; the animals on the grasslands were running away, the high chimneys of the factories were recounting the last incidents, deprived of their glory of smoke, next to windowless buildings; in one corner of the countryside Sparkling thought he saw a dance around a great fire; could it be peasants close to a conflagration? Finally, the train entered the dense moorlands of the land of Thieve.

VI

AT Thieve station landaus were waiting; a cavalry squadron, sabres drawn, was pushing aside a surly and menacing crowd. When the travellers came into view catcalls rang out. Sparkling made clear his desire that no shots should be fired at these humble people. The carriages went through the village at break-neck speed; at the windows women's fists were brandished and coarse rebukes were raining down. It was necessary, at the corner of one street, to clear away a pretence of a barricade; everywhere there was the rumbling of a crowd, unlike that of the already conquered city, but of haggard, ragged, sickly tramps with empty stomachs; thanks to this halt the crowd from the station began to catch up with the rear guard of the escort, and stones started again to alternate with insults. The cortege was finally able to set off and rush into the very long avenue leading to the ceremonial entrance to the castle. Shots were ringing out, first brief, isolated shots, then a whole fusillade ripped though the wind. They spurred on. The castle was being attacked.

The sudden arrival of the horsemen and the coaches created disorder amongst the attackers who were already masters of the outskirts; it was only by using sabre blows that the former managed to enter the main courtyard which straight away, behind them, was filled with the mob of rioters, infuriated peasants brandishing pitchforks, scythes and rifles, shouting for death and pillage. The castle's defenders who were shooting from first-floor windows had stopped firing their muskets for fear of wounding their friends and the Queen, directing them in a manly way, was waiting. Sparkling was holding Christian in his arms, for the King, in his madness, was howling and trying to throw himself among the rebels. They were now in front of the steps to the main entrance and were almost safe.

Then a window opened and there appeared standing, unnoticed in this feverish atmosphere, an unforgettable pale face framed by a thick and wild grey mane; it was the mad Queen, Christian's sister, the unfortunate lunatic who was being looked after in this castle and who, haggard, was looking on without understanding at the funereal sight of Christian, in his madness, coming under the same arches as herself to drag out his incurable existence. She had managed to escape thanks to the disorder; where had she found the rifle that she was holding? It was exactly the same spectacle that she was seeing again, this red spectacle that haunted her fever and the ruins of her brain. The drama was happening again before her eyes: the man held by his arms, in front of the balcony of his Palace surrounded by the crowd, the rifle shots, this sound that she had never been able to forget. She took aim, fired, and Christian, struck down by a bullet to the forehead, collapsed like an empty sack into the arms of Sparkling. And amidst the superhuman terror, the combatants, the King's men, prostrate, and the terrified serfs, saw the mad woman, as if she wanted to carry out a wild pyrrhic victory dance, with an inarticulate cry, leap over the balcony and come, across the empty space, to smash herself alongside the body of Christian and to splatter him with her blood.

At this moment of horrible tragedy the two sides hesitated and the orders to attack only partially started again, except outside the castle where surrounded gendarmes were defending themselves, when a great cry of "every man for himself" punctuated by trumpet sounds rang out and the peasants were fleeing everywhere, dying in all the ditches, pinned by lance thrusts to all the trees, thanks to a sudden cavalry attack. The saviours of the Château de Thieve were horsemen in long cloaks with chapskas on their heads. Their squadrons were roaming over the plain, chasing those fleeing; almost immediately a music of drums, of bugles and of fifes announced the arrival of lines of infantry, in battle order, who were coming to form up in front of the castle. And a few minutes later, the head of Siegfried Gottlob's advance party was coming to bow before Christian's widow and to announce to her the arrival, the very next day, of the Emperor with the forces which should, under his aegis, re-establish, beyond any dispute and any attack, the dynasty of Silberglass that had been so cruelly tested.

And the widow was mourning, and Sparkling and the Duchess were on their knees, weeping, and their comrades from the escort, in desolation, were looking on at the bodies of the two royal victims, stretched out on their divans of death, whilst there could be heard on the road the interminable march past of the infantry of Niederwaldstein, and the silence was only broken by military orders, for the foreign troops as they paraded in front of the castle of mourning were bearing arms to it.

A PARTIAL LIST OF SNUGGLY BOOKS

G. ALBERT AURIER *Elsewhere and Other Stories*
CHARLES BARBARA *My Lunatic Asylum*
S. HENRY BERTHOUD *Misanthropic Tales*
LÉON BLOY *The Desperate Man*
LÉON BLOY *The Tarantulas' Parlor and Other Unkind Tales*
ÉLÉMIR BOURGES *The Twilight of the Gods*
CYRIEL BUYSSE *The Aunts*
JAMES CHAMPAGNE *Harlem Smoke*
FÉLICIEN CHAMPSAUR *The Latin Orgy*
BRENDAN CONNELL *Unofficial History of Pi Wei*
BRENDAN CONNELL *The Metapheromenoi*
RAFAELA CONTRERAS *The Turquoise Ring and Other Stories*
ADOLFO COUVE *When I Think of My Missing Head*
QUENTIN S. CRISP *Aiaigasa*
LADY DILKE *The Outcast Spirit and Other Stories*
CATHERINE DOUSTEYSSIER-KHOZE
  The Beauty of the Death Cap
ÉDOUARD DUJARDIN *Hauntings*
BERIT ELLINGSEN *Now We Can See the Moon*
ERCKMANN-CHATRIAN *A Malediction*
ALPHONSE ESQUIROS *The Enchanted Castle*
ENRIQUE GÓMEZ CARRILLO *Sentimental Stories*
DELPHI FABRICE *The Red Spider*
EDMOND AND JULES DE GONCOURT *Manette Salomon*
REMY DE GOURMONT *From a Faraway Land*
REMY DE GOURMONT *Morose Vignettes*
GUIDO GOZZANO *Alcina and Other Stories*
GUSTAVE GUICHES *The Modesty of Sodom*
EDWARD HERON-ALLEN *The Complete Shorter Fiction*
EDWARD HERON-ALLEN *Three Ghost-Written Novels*
RHYS HUGHES *Cloud Farming in Wales*
J.-K. HUYSMANS *The Crowds of Lourdes*
J.-K. HUYSMANS *Knapsacks*
COLIN INSOLE *Valerie and Other Stories*
JUSTIN ISIS *Pleasant Tales II*

VICTOR JOLY *The Unknown Collaborator and Other Legendary Tales*
MARIE KRYSINSKA *The Path of Amour*
BERNARD LAZARE *The Mirror of Legends*
BERNARD LAZARE *The Torch-Bearers*
MAURICE LEVEL *The Shadow*
JEAN LORRAIN *Errant Vice*
JEAN LORRAIN *Fards and Poisons*
JEAN LORRAIN *Masks in the Tapestry*
JEAN LORRAIN *Monsieur de Bougrelon and Other Stories*
JEAN LORRAIN *Nightmares of an Ether-Drinker*
JEAN LORRAIN *The Soul-Drinker and Other Decadent Fantasies*
ARTHUR MACHEN *N*
ARTHUR MACHEN *Ornaments in Jade*
CAMILLE MAUCLAIR *The Frail Soul and Other Stories*
CATULLE MENDÈS *Bluebirds*
CATULLE MENDÈS *For Reading in the Bath*
CATULLE MENDÈS *Mephistophela*
ÉPHRAÏM MIKHAËL *Halyartes and Other Poems in Prose*
LUIS DE MIRANDA *Who Killed the Poet?*
OCTAVE MIRBEAU *The Death of Balzac*
CHARLES MORICE *Babels, Balloons and Innocent Eyes*
GABRIEL MOUREY *Monada*
DAMIAN MURPHY *Daughters of Apostasy*
KRISTINE ONG MUSLIM *Butterfly Dream*
CHARLES NODIER *Outlaws and Sorrows*
HERSH DOVID NOMBERG *A Cheerful Soul and Other Stories*
PHILOTHÉE O'NEDDY *The Enchanted Ring*
YARROW PAISLEY *Mendicant City*
URSULA PFLUG *Down From*
JEREMY REED *When a Girl Loves a Girl*
JEREMY REED *Bad Boys*
ADOLPHE RETTÉ *Misty Thule*
JEAN RICHEPIN *The Bull-Man and the Grasshopper*
DAVID RIX *A Blast of Hunters*
FREDERICK ROLFE (Baron Corvo) *Amico di Sandro*
JASON ROLFE *An Archive of Human Nonsense*
ARNAUD RYKNER *The Last Train*

MARCEL SCHWOB *The Assassins and Other Stories*
MARCEL SCHWOB *Double Heart*
CHRISTIAN HEINRICH SPIESS *The Dwarf of Westerbourg*
BRIAN STABLEFORD (editor)
  Decadence and Symbolism: A Showcase Anthology
BRIAN STABLEFORD (editor) *The Snuggly Satyricon*
BRIAN STABLEFORD (editor) *The Snuggly Satanicon*
BRIAN STABLEFORD *Spirits of the Vasty Deep*
COUNT ERIC STENBOCK *Love, Sleep & Dreams*
COUNT ERIC STENBOCK *Myrtle, Rue & Cypress*
COUNT ERIC STENBOCK *The Shadow of Death*
COUNT ERIC STENBOCK *Studies of Death*
MONTAGUE SUMMERS *The Bride of Christ and Other Fictions*
MONTAGUE SUMMERS *Six Ghost Stories*
GILBERT-AUGUSTIN THIERRY *The Blonde Tress and The Mask*
GILBERT-AUGUSTIN THIERRY *Reincarnation and Redemption*
DOUGLAS THOMPSON *The Fallen West*
TOADHOUSE *Gone Fishing with Samy Rosenstock*
TOADHOUSE *Living and Dying in a Mind Field*
TOADHOUSE *What Makes the Wave Break?*
LÉO TRÉZENIK *Decadent Prose Pieces*
RUGGERO VASARI *Raun*
ILARIE VORONCA *The Confession of a False Soul*
JANE DE LA VAUDÈRE *The Demi-Sexes and The Androgynes*
JANE DE LA VAUDÈRE *The Double Star and Other Occult Fantasies*
JANE DE LA VAUDÈRE *The Mystery of Kama and Brahma's Courtesans*
JANE DE LA VAUDÈRE *Three Flowers and The King of Siam's Amazon*
JANE DE LA VAUDÈRE *The Witch of Ecbatana and The Virgin of Israel*
AUGUSTE VILLIERS DE L'ISLE-ADAM *Isis*
RENÉE VIVIEN AND HÉLÈNE DE ZUYLEN DE NYEVELT
  Faustina and Other Stories
RENÉE VIVIEN *Lilith's Legacy*
RENÉE VIVIEN *A Woman Appeared to Me*
ILARIE VORONKA *The Confession of a False Soul*
TERESA WILMS MONTT *In the Stillness of Marble*
TERESA WILMS MONTT *Sentimental Doubts*
KAREL VAN DE WOESTIJNE *The Dying Peasant*

www.ingramcontent.com/pod-product-compliance
Lightning Source LLC
LaVergne TN
LVHW041630060526
838200LV00040B/1512